NUMBER 96

Edited by

John P. Gunnison

© 2007 Adventure House

THE BLACKOUT MURDERS, SNATCHERS ARE SUCKERS, A GRAVE FOR GROGAN Black Book Detective, March 1942. Copyright © 1942 by Better Publications, Inc.

Subscription Rate - $45.00 - 1 Year (6 Issues) - Advertising Rates - Full Page - $75.00. The publisher has made every effort to contact the present owners of any copyrighted material. Our apologies to those who hold such rights but whom we failed to contact because ownership was unknown or addresses were incomplete. Appropriate credit will be given in future editions if such copyright holders contact the publisher.

Printed in the United States of America

ISBN-13: 978-1-59798-130-9
ISBN: 1-59798-130-3

First Adventure House Edition September 2007

Every pulp had a letters column, well those that lasted longer than a single or two issues that is. Most nearly every character pulp had not only a standard letters column, but also had a department for its readers. This department would garner interest on upcoming stories, solicit clubs readers could join and for a modern reader a window on history past. BLACK BOOK DETECTIVE was no different and their department was titled, OFF THE RECORD. Here is part of the column that appeared in this issue of BLACK BOOK DETECTIVE that we are reprinting here:

AMERICA AT WAR - As we write this, America has awakened and is presenting a united front against war that is no longer a threat but a reality. The story in this present issue of the BLACK BOOK DETECTIVE that you now hold in your hands is especially timely, for our great cities have known and still know the threat of air raids of war as they have never experienced before. And in knowing, we are all united and ready for whatever there is to come. To face our problems valiantly as one nation and one people fighting for a common goal. In BLACK BOOK DETECTIVE we will strive to present the kind of fiction that will prove relaxing in the midst of our tense activity—and all our novels and short stories, will, as ever, reflect the patriotism and honor that is in the heart of every good American.

Pulps were then and just as importantly now a window through which America could be seen. It's fears, and hopes. How did "The Greatest Generation" cope with their stress. That stress that began with the depression and continued on into World War II. That generation's choices for entertainment was severely limited compared to what we have today. Movies, radio, newspapers, hardback books, slick magazines, comics and pulps were the choices for those with a dime or two in their pockets. Comics were becoming more and more popular, but the cost of production was high compared to the pulps, and nearly every pulp publisher was also a comic publisher. We hope you'll enjoy this first post Pearl Harbor Black Bat story.

Happy Reading

John P. Gunnison
gunnison@adventurehouse.com

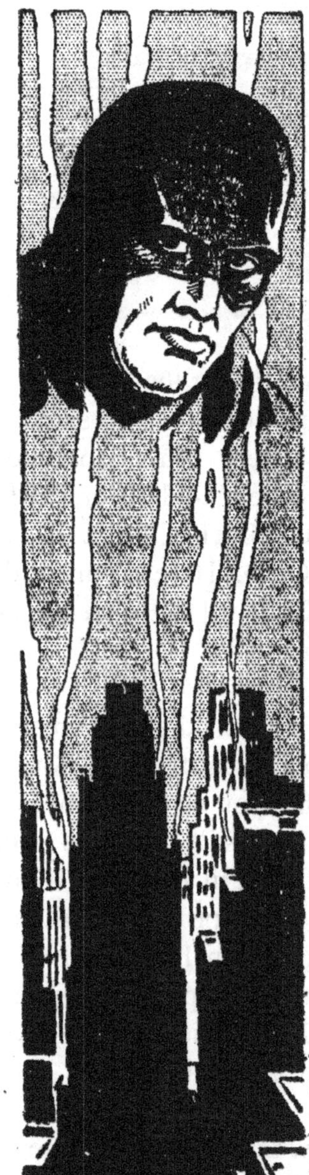

In the spot where he had been was a tower of

THE BLACKOUT

CHAPTER I

Escape to Death

THERE was a certain measure of excitement prevailing over the blackout of New York City, scheduled for ten o'clock. Everyone wanted to see how Times Square, the fashionable avenues, and the down-town cut-rate shops would look completely inked out.

Fireworks were promised, too, for after flights of Army and Navy planes studied the blackout from the air, three big reconnaissance bombers were to streak across the city, drop flares that would create millions of candle power and photograph the

flames and fury (Chaper I)

MURDERS By G. WAYMAN JONES

area with cameras synchronized with the explosion of the flares.

Every police officer was on duty and under orders to keep a watchful eye for crime which might spring up during the half hour of pitch darkness. Radio cars, with taped headlamps and special blue bulbs would criss-cross the main arteries and side streets and, for those thirty minutes, be the only moving traffic on the streets.

All this brought the war closer than ever, and precautions were necessary. Air Raid Wardens would be at their posts, fire houses and hospitals on the alert.

Steps had been taken to simulate actual air-raid conditions as closely as possible. Everything would be there—save the bombs.

Twenty minutes before the zero hour, traffic already was subsiding. Hotel windows were draped with black curtains, apartment houses were prepared to throw switches to darken every room.

In one of the poorer sections of the city were three large tenement houses, now abandoned and ready for wrecking crews. They were close together, with narrow, dismal alleys between them. Nobody on the streets noticed a window being slowly opened on the second floor of the middle building. A man—his features harrowed by terror, ducked his head out and looked around. He turned pale when he saw the distance to the cement paved alley, but there was little hesitation on his part.

HE THRUST one leg over the window sill and sat astride it for a moment while he looked up and down the alley below him. Certain he was unobserved, the man secured a hold on the sill with his fingers and let himself drop down. Apparently he overestimated the strength in his fingers for—as the full weight of his body came down on them—they slipped and let go. He dropped like a leaden weight hit the pavement and lay there for a few seconds.

With a great effort that must have been induced by some compelling reason, he got to his feet, took a couple of forward steps and fell again.

He reached his feet once more and leaned weakly against the brick wall. Then he started limping forward. Every few steps he'd look over his shoulder as though he expected grim shadows to spring out of the darkness upon him. The man obviously was frightened and just as obviously determined.

When he reached the mouth of the alley, he saw a taxi roll smoothly down the street. He waved frantically, and the cab pulled into the curb. The man limped toward it, wincing with each step. He got the door open and tumbled into the tonneau.

"The airport—as fast as you can travel!" he gasped to the driver. "The one where those photographic planes are ready to take off. Hurry!"

The driver grimaced.

"Can't do it, pal. In twenty minutes there's gonna be a blackout and nothin' can move, y'see? It'll take me pretty near that time to reach the field. Or wait—things are quieting down. Maybe I could make it."

"Fifty dollars if you do—but hurry. This is a matter of life and death. If I fail to reach the airport in time, twelve men will die. Can't use the telephone because they'd never believe me. Will you please get started?"

The driver seemed to realize the seriousness of all this. He shifted into gear and shot away, taking the next corner on two wheels. As he suspected, traffic had all but stopped already. He skipped through several lights, made expert turns against others and soon crossed the Queensborough Bridge. The airport was only a short distance away now—but the minutes were passing rapidly.

The driver squirmed around in his seat and spoke without taking eyes off the road.

"You ain't thinkin' about going into the airport, pal? They got marines posted all around the place. If you try it, they might take a pot shot at you."

"I'll risk that—only hurry! Hurry!"

The driver shrugged and opened his cab wide. Soon they saw the lights of the airport—which were due to wink out in just two minutes. The injured man kept massaging his swollen ankle. It gave him something to do—something which took

middle-aged passenger, "it's impossible to get by those babies at the gate. Nobody is allowed on the field for the next hour or so."

"Help me," the passenger, groaned as he put weight on his injured ankle. "They *can't* stop me, I tell you!

THE BLACK BAT

his mind off the grim tragedy that impended.

The cab rolled up fairly close to the gate. Two marines were on duty with bayoneted rifles. The cab driver got out and opened the car door.

"I'm telling you," he warned the

Absolutely nothing *must* stop me!"

The cab driver helped him up to the gate, where the two marines instantly challenged them. Before any explanations could be offered, the zero hour was at hand. Every light winked out, and the roar of big bombing planes broke the moment of silence.

"Let me by," the injured man pleaded. "I've got to reach those planes."

The marine sentries, momentarily blinded by the sudden darkness and partly deafened from the big plane motors, blundered against one another. The cab driver raced back to his taxi. The injured man ducked low, passed the sentries and then started a limping run across the field. He waved his hands and shouted at the top of his voice.

SOMEONE must have heard him, because a searchlight swept the field, picked him out and centered on him. He was a wild looking specimen, hair rumpled, hat missing, clothes grimy and torn. The look on his face could easily have been mistaken for mad hatred instead of the horror that shone there.

Several men started running toward him. Then it happened. The searchlight made it impossible for those who witnessed the event, not to believe their own eyes. They last saw the man, arms raised high, voice yelling something indistinguishable. Then, in the spot where he had been, was a tall tower of flame and fury. Debris shot skyward, a crater appeared mysteriously, as if someone had dug it from below the ground.

After the blast, the concussion set in as air rushed to occupy the vacuum caused by the explosive. Trees swayed wildly. Two light planes, not far away, were half turned around by the force of the air currents. The sound went roaring into space, almost shattering the ear drums of the witnesses.

Those who finally reached the spot, now bathed in the glare of half a dozen big searchlights, found very little to indicate that a human being had been there only a moment before. There were a shoe, somehow intact, a few bits of clothing and buttons.

Colonel Whately, in charge of the photography flight, yelled orders. Field lights came on. The two sentries were running up, panting, barely able to talk.

"He got by us when the blackout came," one gasped. "He was crazy as a bug, sir. Kept saying he had to reach the reconnaissance planes."

"Get back to your posts," Whately ordered. "And close the gates too.

We're going ahead with the plans as before. Nobody gets in—reporters or anyone else. Watch yourselves, now. That's all."

Whately turned to several officials of the field who stood gaping at the whole in the ground.

"It's rather evident," Whately explained, "that this man, whoever he was, came here with the intentions of sabotage. He was carrying a bomb which he hoped to use on the photography planes. He must have overestimated the time fuse, and it went off before he could put the thing to its intended use."

"Thank heavens for that," one man sighed. "He might have killed a lot of people. I—uh—hardly suppose he'll ever be identified."

"Hardly!" Whately said. "Now please get back to your posts I'm going to have the planes checked before they take off. Never expected any sabotaging of this plan—seems utterly nonsensical, but saboteurs think strangely at times."

WHATELY gave the necessary orders, and a dozen men went over the three big bombers with finetooth combs. Every nook and corner of them was examined until even Whately expressed complete satisfaction that no nefarious machines could be hidden in them.

Three men came out of one hangar, each carrying a bulky box-like affair—the valuable cameras which would photograph New York City while it was under complete blackout. These were installed in the planes by experts. The flares were checked, and crews took into their specified positions.

Radio messages from the bombers, now flying above the city, indicated that the blackout test was highly satisfactory. Then came word for the photography planes to take off. Each contained four men—two pilots, the photographer and a radio operator. They swung into position for the takeoff and then, one by one, roared down the field. Breaking contact with the ground, they nosed toward the stars.

Colonel Whately stood in the darkness, watching them fade from sight. He bit at his lower lip.

"My prayers go with them," he said softly. "I'm not given to hunches, but there's a premonition in my heart. I can't get it out no matter how hard I try."

"Nonsense," another officer laughed. "What could happen to them? The destruction of a saboteur by his own bomb was rather a ghastly business. Thank heavens, it destroyed him and not what his bomb was meant for."

But Colonel Whately's premonition was right. Those three reconnaissance bombers, now heading for the center of the city, were doomed. The men who flew them had no more chance than a convicted murderer, strapped in the electric chair. New York was going to get some fireworks all right— but far more furious fireworks than its citizens expected.

CHAPTER II

Oblivion

ON the West Side of town, among the stately mansions lining one of the most exclusive sections, was a large dwelling, set back from the street like its neighbors. Trees and carefully cultivated shrubs completely shrouded it from its neighbor to the north. On the south side of the house was a cross street.

A neat iron gate offered admittance, and beside it was a brass nameplate indicating that this was the residence of Anthony Quinn.

At this particular moment every light was out, in accordance with the requests of authorities in charge of the blackout. Tony Quinn and his man of all trades, Silk Kirby, were both in the spacious garden behind the house.

Tony Quinn was tall, rugged looking, and at one time he might have been handsome. Now there were deep, ugly scars burned into the flesh around his eyes. Those eyes were blank and lifeless too. He used a cane with which to feel his way along, although Silk Kirby was at his side to guide him.

Silk looked something like his nickname. He was bald, about forty, and slender. But he had a polished way about him, one calculated to arouse the greatest confidence in others, even strangers. Silk had worked hard to acquire that polish, and it served him well when he had been one of the smartest confidence men in the country.

"I think, sir," Silk looked around, "we're quite safe. The trees and shrubs, together with the blackout, won't permit anyone to see you."

Quinn nodded. Those dead eyes of his suddenly were alive. It was a miraculous change and, so far as Tony Quinn was concerned, an actual miracle, too.

"We're getting a taste of what war will be like if we get into it," he said in a pleasant voice. "Listen—the planes are coming over. I can also see them about a dozen bombers simulating an attack. Now the fighting planes are sweeping in to meet them. They're really doing it up brown, Silk."

Silk tried to penetrate the gloom. He shook his head slowly.

"So you can even see the planes way up there. I must say, sir, that you have been repaid with interest for your months of real blindness."

Quinn smiled.

"Yes, Silk. Darkness means nothing to me. I can even see colors in a pitch black room. . . . Now the bombers have been theoretically driven off. The photography planes are coming in. They'll drop flares and take pictures of the city. If any land near us—within a quarter of a mile—keep your eyes closed. They are extremely bright things. The planes are gaining altitude. They'll let the flares go at any moment now."

Suddenly the blackness was illuminated by an intense, blinding light from a dozen big flares. At that precise instant there were three distinct flashes of crimson—high in the sky. Quinn gave a sharp cry of horror.

"Silk! The planes! They've exploded in midair! I saw them one moment—and the next there was only the flash of three bombs. They exploded simultaneously. Silk! That was murder! Sabotage!"

"But how?" Silk gaped.

"If one of the planes had blown to bits it might have been accidental, but when three of them are blasted at the same split second, that's no accident, Silk. Let's go back into the house and listen for radio reports on what happened."

THEY ran lightly toward the back door. Suddenly street lights came one, house windows were lit again. Tony Quinn slowed up abruptly, his eyes blank and blind once more. He tapped his cane as he walked along, with Silk guiding him. They climbed the stairs tot he back door and went in. Even here, within the privacy of his home, Tony Quinn continued to carry out his pose as a blind man.

He went into his study, sat down in a deep, worn and comfortable leather chair in front of the fireplace and reached for pipe and tobacco, fumbling across the top of the small table beside the chair. Silk snapped on the radio. He turned the dial, but apparently news rooms hadn't released the story of destruction in the sky as yet.

While they waited, Quinn sucked impatiently on his pipe. Those eyes of his were filmed over, and he stared at a blank wall. Yet the same eyes had been able to penetrate the inky darkness, a mile in the sky, and watch the maneuvers of the planes.

Tony Quinn had once been a fighting young district attorney, earnestly engaged in cleaning up crime. Then, one day in open court, crooks had attempted to destroy evidence by hurling acid upon it. In the struggle, Tony Quinn received the contents of an acid bottle squarely in the eyes. He'd gone blind instantly.

Wealthy enough to retain the best eye surgeons in the world, he had traveled extensively, seeking one man who would say there was a chance. But none did. So far as the world in general was concerned, Tony Quinn was blinded for life.

Just before the catastrophe, Silk Kirby had appeared. He'd slipped into Quinn's home to rob it, but by a lucky coincidence had saved Quinn's life from murdering gangsters. Silk had remained with him then and when Quinn became blind, he proved an indispensable aide.

One night, months after he'd gone blind, a girl appeared at his home. She was Carol Baldwin, whose father lay dying in a midwestern town, the victim of a gangster's bullet. Carol came with a strange proposition, inspired by her father. As a police official, he'd fought crime tooth and nail until finally it caught up with him. He knew of Tony Quinn, had followed his spectacular career and recognized in him potentialities that might prove useful in the everlasting battle against criminals.

Tony Quinn, grasping at straws, had gone willingly with Carol to this small town. There, a little known surgeon had performed a miracle. He transplanted parts of Carol's father's eyes into Tony Quinn's head. Carol's father died soon after, and then there were weeks of indescribable suspense when Tony Quinn wondered if he would see when the bandages were removed.

He did see—with a sight more profound than any other man. Nature

Roughhands pushed Silk beneath the waters. In a few minutes he would be dead (Chapter XIV)

had repaid him for those dismal days of darkness. He could see in the night —penetrate the inky blackness as easily as the average man sees by day. Not only that—during his blindness nature had also recompensed him by adding to his sense of touch, hearing and smell. These improved faculties remained with him.

He saw Carol Baldwin, too, in all her blond beauty. They made plans— and so the Black Bat was created. Wearing a hood that covered his face and hid those telltale scars, a cape which was ribbed like the wings of a bat, Tony Quinn challenged the underworld. Soon his name became the most dreaded word uttered in the dens where crime was hatched.

HE OPERATED in a wholly unorthodox manner, without heed to laws and rules. The police sought him because—when it was necessary —the Black Bat's twin automatics spat death. He always branded his victims with a small sticker in the form of a bat so that no one else would be blamed for the killings.

Gradually the reputation of the Black Bat reached the far corners of the globe, and those men who moved in the shadows of guilt, cowered when he stepped into the game. There was a price on his head, and thousands of crooks willingly would have tried to collect it save that the Black Bat shot faster and vanished more completely than any other man alive.

Jack O'Leary, known better as Butch, was the fourth member of the little organization working with the Black Bat. Butch was a huge, slow-thinking man who had often proved his worth. He had hands like hams, a bull neck and a mild disposition until crossed. Then he became a human tornado of action and strength.

Others might suspect that blind Tony Quinn was the Black Bat, but there were not many who could reconcile themselves to believing that a man pronounced incurably blind by famous doctors was the Black Bat. The most prominent exception was Captain McGrath of the Police Department. He had sworn to arrest the Black Bat, and he strongly suspected that Tony Quinn and the Black Bat were synonymous.

All his efforts to prove this had been in vain, although several times Captain McGrath had no idea how close he'd come. McGrath was honest, efficient and capable. Tony Quinn liked him despite the manner in which he thrust himself into cases and sought to corner the Black Bat. That was McGrath's job.

Police Commissioner Warner, long a friend of Tony Quinn, also may have possessed an inkling, but even if Warner could prove the fact, he never would have done so. The Black Bat worked on the side of law and order. He broke open some of the toughest cases Warner had ever known. Yet, because of his methods, the Black Bat was subject to instant arrest if caught. This only lent more spice to the game so far as Tony Quinn was concerned.

He'd gone back into private law practice recently because it helped to relieve the boredom between cases and also provided him with an open method of investigating certain circumstances connected with the various cases. He maintained an office downtown and was creating a substantial practice.

NOW Tony Quinn waited impatiently for the first news flash. It came but it was brief because facts were not known. Every person in those three planes had been blown into eternity. Even the planes were reduced to slivers of wood and hunks of metal. Sabotage was suspected, and the complete story of the man who was blown to bits by his own bomb also was made public.

Silk shut off the radio. Quinn leaned back with a frown.

"Ghastly business—but interesting from our angle, eh, Silk? It does look like the work of saboteurs, but could it be? Why did they destroy those three planes when they might have done a great deal more damage with the larger and newer bombers that simulated an attack on the city? It doesn't make sense.

"Then too, the man who was blown to bits at the airport—that isn't logical, either. Saboteurs know their business. They'd hardly flop on something like that. And, while we're theorizing, why should preparations be made to blow up the planes when they were in the air while other plans indicated they were to be destroyed on the ground?"

"Yes, sir," Silk said hopefully. "Do you think it might be something for the—ah—Black Bat to look into, sir? We've been idle for several weeks

now. Doesn't do a man good to get stale, sir."

Quinn smiled slowly.

"No matter what it is, Silk, we know someone has performed wholesale murder. All of which does interest the Black Bat. It just occurred to me that a man named Joel King was in the news lately just a casual mention. He's an inventor and has claimed to have been hard at work on some device with which he hopes to be able to explode muntions dumps, gasoline supplies and even bombs on the racks of military planes."

Silk laughed.

"The good old death ray stuff?"

"No," Quinn was serious. "Joel King is, or was, no fool. He was graduated from good schools and has done splendid work in the past. Two weeks ago he mysteriously dropped out of sight. The usual conjecture, that he overworked himself and is suffering from amnesia, has been advanced. Maybe it's true."

Silk's smile faded.

"What if he did perfect something, and he's trying it out? Some of those inventors are half crazy, anyway."

"Not Joel King," Quinn contradicted. "I've been interested in his disappearance because it resembled another case on which we worked—one where a master crook kidnaped inventors and forced them to divulge what they knew and then stole their ideas.

"I doubt that anyone else is trying that trick, but suppose people hostile to this country and democracy in general have snatched him, have taken his device and are using it here? Such an instrument in the wrong hands would create havoc we have never before known. I—"

Silk was suddenly alert.

"The new device we rigged up to announce the presence of somebody in the laboratory, just worked. It must be either Carol or Butch."

"Draw the shades," Quinn instructed. "I'll go in. You stay here and keep watch."

Silk drew the shades. Quinn arose, tapped his way across the room and then dropped the pose of a blind man. He thrust the cane under one arm, operated hidden controls on the wall and a section of book shelf slid away to reveal the entrance of a perfectly concealed laboratory which was the Black Bat's workshop.

On top of one bookcase section was a stuffed owl. Silk had noticed one of its eyes glow a soft green. It was the signal that the lab was occupied.

Only two people, besides Tony Quinn and Silk knew how to reach the lab. Carol or Butch had to dodge through the garden gate entrance to Quinn's estate, cross a dark area of trees and plants and then enter the garden house far behind Quinn's residence. A trap door opened into a tunnel which, in turn, led directly to the lab.

Butch was the visitor, and he seemed greatly agitated. The moment the door slid shut, he lumbered forward. He was almost tall enough to reach the ceiling, and his bulk actually filled a good portion of the room itself. Butch held a phonograph record in one hand.

"Boss," he said excitedly, "I was downtown, see? Them big planes blew up like you must know about by now. Well, a guy comes up to me and hands me this phonograph record. He says it's free for nothing and I should take it home and play it. He handed out a lot of them to other people."

"Did you play it?" Quinn asked.

"Sure! It was free, and I figured maybe it had a hot tune on it. So I went home, put it on my little radio phonograph and—boss—you gotta listen to it yourself. You gotta—because I only understand part of it."

QUINN took the recording and placed it on a portable machine which formed part of his laboratory equipment.

The record started off with a song and then suddenly broke off while a sinister, crafty voice spoke.

"My dear listener: You know what happened to those three planes during the blackout. You know what happened to a man who was rushing across the airport field. Those were not accidents nor acts of sabotage, but a warning and a lesson. I have perfected a means of destroying anything or everything on earth. The use of this device will make the United States undoubted master of the world —stop this war instantly.

"You wonder why I do not present it to our government? Because I have spent money and time on it. The government would hardly pay my price once they knew its secret and they wouldn't even negotiate until they did know its construction. Therefore, I take this means of informing you, a citizen of the United States, that for twenty million dollars your government may purchase my apparatus.

"Twenty million dollars—a vast sum, but paltry in view of what it will buy—the means of stopping wars forever. At the present time I have nothing further to say, but I shall contact many of you again in the near future. Think it over. Twenty million dollars for the greatest instrument ever created by man.

Then the music came on again and played to a finish.

Tony Quinn's eyes were alive and sparkling. He looked at Butch.

"It was come about as I expected. Butch the Black Bat is going to fly again—to operate against the greatest menace we've ever known—a man in possession of an instrument that can deal wholesale death. This is not the theoretical death ray of fiction, but an actual fact, scientifically composed.

"Such an invention has been worked on for years. Now it is perfected and in the hands of a man who would blackmail the nation for its secret. Not only that—the man is an out-and-out murderer. The death of the unknown at the airport now is proven to be murder.

"These phonograph records must have been made long before it happened so the person behind this mad scheme knew the mysterious victim at the airport was going to die—even knew the manner of his death. We're not fighting a stupid individual, Butch."

"Yeah," Butch's big hands curled into massive fists. "I'd like to bust him one. He's a real patriot, ain't he? I'll turn him into a dead one. Just say the word, boss. I'm ready for action."

CHAPTER III

Welcome Client

TONY QUINN, eyes blank and dead, sat behind his desk in the private office of his law suite. Silk sat in a corner, ready to help his blind employer when his services were required. Quinn's mind wasn't on his work this morning. He could still see those three planes as they burst into little pieces high up the sky. He could still hear that sneering, calculating voice from the phonograph record, preparing everyone for that demand upon the government for a huge fortune in cash.

The annunciator buzzed. Quinn's clerk in the outer office announced that Police Commissioner Warner and a girl were waiting to see him. Quinn ordered them in at once and arose with his right hand outstretched somewhat vaguely in the general direction of the door.

Commissioner Warner, tall, militarily erect, grey haired and the best Commissioner of Police the city had ever had, grasped Tony Quinn's hand.

"I hope I'm not disturbing you, Tony," he said, "but I've brought along a client."

"Well, thanks," Quinn smiled. He could see the girl—obviously somewhat frightened, but red-haired and distractingly pretty. "Won't both of you sit down?"

They did, and Warner nodded pleasantly in Silk's direction before he explained the reason for his coming.

"This very pretty young lady beside me is Viola King. Her father disappeared about a month ago. The case is in the Missing Persons Bureau now. Miss King came to see me and explained that her father's mysterious disappearance had left her somewhat embarrassed financially, that he had money, but she couldn't touch it. As an attorney, you can figure ways and means of providing her with the money Joel King left when he vanished."

"Of course," Quinn said, and his calm manner indicated none of the excitement that seethed in his brain.

This was the daughter of Joel King —the man who might have invented a device by which planes and even men could be blown to bits. Through her he might get at the truth of this affair. It was a made-to-order case —and probably the deliberate work of Commissioner Warner, who may have hoped the Black Bat would become interested.

The girl was making mincemeat out of a handkerchief between her fingers.

"Mr. Quinn—that isn't quite all. Dad wasn't sick. He couldn't have forgotten who he was. He—he's dead. I *know* he's dead. Hank doesn't think so, but—"

"Who is Hank?" Quinn asked soothingly.

"He's Hank Standish. We were going to be married when this happened. Hank says he just got lost and will turn up soon. But it's almost a whole month."

"Miss King," Quinn said. "I'll get to work at once. Would you mind waiting in another office. Silk, please—"

SILK escorted her out of the room. Quinn leaned across his desk. His eyes were directed about three feet to Commissioner Warner's left.

"Commissioner—in view of what happened last night—I'm just wondering a bit."

Warner smiled.

"Exactly what I hoped you'd do. A man of your brains, Tony, could help us in this case. That was murder last night. You've heard about the phonograph records distributed all around the city? That's proof of it.

Now—what's on your mind?"

"From the very meager description of the man who was blown up at the airport I'm wondering if it could possibly have been Joel King. I spent a lot of time thinking this over last night. Silk faithfully reads all the newspapers to me, and I have a retentive brain. It has little else to do but absorb what I hear.

"Now Joel King was an inventor who professed to be working on a device which could do to planes exactly what happened to those three. Joel King has disappeared, so what's the logical line of reasoning?"

Warner pulled his chair closer and dropped his voice.

"Tony, I'm going to be very frank. As District Attorney you showed the shrewd mind you possess. Certain people believe you are the Black Bat. For my part I'm on the fence between doubt and theory.

"I hope you are the Black Bat— which is a funny thing for a Police Commissioner to say, especially since a warrant is in my drawer calling for the Black Bat's arrest."

"We've been through all that before," Quinn said. "I'm stone blind, Warner. How *could* I be the Black Bat? Go on talking."

"I brought Viola King here deliberately because she offers a clue to this greatest of mysteries—the destruction of a man isolated in the middle of a wide open air field and the simultaneous destruction of three big bombing planes in the air.

"From what we have pieced together, a taxi driver tells us that he picked up this mystery man who died at the airport, just twenty minutes before blackout time. A sentry at the airport noted the marker number of the cab, and we picked up the driver.

"He was offered fifty dollars to get the man to the airport before those three planes took off. The man vaguely answers the description of Joel King. The taxi driver says that the man was injured—seemed to be limping badly, that his clothes were covered with dirt as though he'd fallen."

"Hm," Quinn mused. "Interesting. The man obviously was injured from a fall of some kind. Therefore we can assume that he did not travel very far before he reached your taxi driver's cab. It's an angle to consider, but not for me. I'm only interested in locating the father of my new client. Could you get that taxi driver over here so I might question him a bit?"

Warner picked up the phone on Quinn's desk, called headquarters and gave orders that the taxi driver was to be brought over at once.

"His name is Steve Cobb, and we're holding him temporarily," Warner explained. "He's innocent, of course, but the only witness we have. I had some men go over the area surrounding the crater which was left by the blast. They didn't find much. A shoe was blasted off the poor devil's foot, but it gives us no clue.

"I'll turn it over to the labs after the medical examiner releases it. Together with a few other bits of cloth and buttons, the shoe is at the morgue —had to be taken here for the medical examination. Foolish, but the doctor was insistent about it."

"While you're here, write me an order to see what was left of that man. See?" Quinn chuckled. "Oh yes, I still talk that way. Hope forever burns in a man's heart. I'll see the remains through the tips of my fingers."

WARNER wrote the necessary order and rose.

"I've got to go back. This business has the whole department on its toes, and the city is flooded with F.B.I. men. I only wish the Black Bat would take a hand in it. I've more faith in him than any other agency."

Quinn laughed softly.

"If he happens to fly in my window, I'll tell him, commissioner, and don't think I'm not envious of him

SILK

either. Thanks for bringing me my client. All I shall do on this case is try to ascertain whether or not the dead man was her father and see to it that she can get at the money in his name."

Twenty minutes later two detectives brought in the taxi driver. Quinn studied the man, although nobody present in the office would have thought so because Quinn's eyes never rested upon him. Quinn sent for Viola King and had her sit down.

"I asked you to come in, Miss King, because I want you to hear a description. It's possible that this cab driver may have seen your father last night. Go ahead, Mr. Cobb. What did this man look like?"

The driver dry-washed his hands nervously.

"Well—I really didn't get so much of a look at the guy. He was maybe fifty or sixty. Had grey hair."

"His nose," Viola King broke in. "Was it long and narrow? Father had a long nose."

"No, ma'am. This guy just had an ordinary nose and kinda red cheeks. His ears stuck out a little bit too, and he had on a brown suit."

Viola King leaned back slowly.

"That wasn't my father. He never had a brown suit, and his cheeks weren't red. His ears didn't stick out either. It wasn't Dad, thank heavens."

The taxi driver stepped closer.

"Say, mister," he addressed Quinn. "I'm in a bad spot, see? If I helped you out any, how about you gettin' me outa this jam? I ain't done nuthin' except give this guy a ride for which I never got paid either, and he promised me fifty bucks. Will you give me a hand, mister? I need a mouthpiece bad."

Quinn smiled.

"Clients simply are pouring in this morning. All right—I'll see what I can do, but of course you'll be required to answer any questions the Police and F.B.I. agents may ask."

"Okay. My pals call me Stevie, and that goes for you, mister. Thanks a million. I'll do anythin' you say."

After Steve Cobb and his detective

escort had gone, Quinn arose. Keeping his fingertips lightly pressed against the surface of his desk, he followed the edge of it until he stood directly in front of Viola King.

"Sometimes," he said, "men like that taxi driver are apt to make up descriptions. Not intentionally, but we can't take any chances. Last night a man was killed—literally blown apart by some death dealing device hurled at him or by a bomb he was carrying. Your father worked on a machine meant to destroy engines and gasoline supplies, didn't he?"

"Why yes, he did. I really don't know how far he progressed because he wouldn't talk about it even to me. Mr. Quinn—you don't think my father had anything to do with the destruction of those planes last night? He couldn't do such a thing. You wouldn't accuse him of that if you knew him. He was always gentle and kind."

"I'm sure he was," Quinn soothed her. "I merely wished to learn more about him. Now suppose we go down to the morgue. It isn't a very pleasant place for a girl. However, there are some remains—clothing—of the man who was killed last night. In order not to take any chances, I think you should look at them. Do you mind?"

"No." Her head came up resolutely. "If Dad is dead, I'd prefer to know it. I'll do whatever you say, Mr. Quinn. I'm ready now."

Silk drove them to the morgue and helped Quinn inside. Quinn presented Commissioner Warner's order to a clerk and received a carton containing a few envelopes of scanty bits of debris and one shoe, unmarked and undamaged. Quinn drew papers from his pocket, laid them on the counter and removed a mechanical pencil from his vest pocket. He retracted the point into its cylinder and then fumbled for the shoe.

"No!" Viola gasped in relief. "No, that isn't Dad's shoe. He wore only old-fashioned high ones and never owned a pair of brown shoes in his life. The size is different, too—much bigger than what he wore."

"Good," Quinn said and laid the shoe down directly upon the papers he'd spread out as if to take notes. Idly the metal point of his pencil prodded at the instep. His fingers lightly dusted over the sole of the shoe and encountered small, very hard particles. Talking, to divert attention from his hands, Quinn managed to dislodge dirt from the instep and also to remove some of those hard particles from the sole. They fell onto the paper.

He handed back the shoe to the clerk, picked up the papers and slowly folded them. His movements were casual, and nobody suspected what he'd removed from that shoe, probably was the only clue this case offered.

"Be glad then, that this man wasn't your father," he told Viola. "We'll drop you at your house now, and I'll get a court order on your bank so money can be withdrawn from your father's account. Will you take my arm? It isn't very often I have the privilege of being escorted by a pretty girl. She *is* pretty, isn't she, Silk?"

"As a picture," Silk opined. "I wish you could see her, sir."

CHAPTER IV

The Black Bat Moves in

AFTER dark, in the privacy of Tony Quinn's hidden laboratory, the Black Bat's crew assembled. Carol Baldwin sat beside Tony Quinn on a davenport. She was blond, blue-eyed and beautiful enough to make any man's head turn as he passed by. Butch straddled a straight-backed chair while Silk remained near the door beside a light which signaled when anyone approached the house or the phone rang.

"Whoever is behind this scheme is, above all, not stupid," said Quinn. "The manner by which he operates shows ingenuity. He knows very well that a demand for twenty million dollars would never be met. Yet his product is well worth that sum if he can get it.

"However, he has resorted to murder, which means he will be hunted down even if the government does dicker with him. The man can't be such a fool as to not realize this. So why in the world did he resort to murder in the first place? Unless— he wants to impress someone else— a foreign power, perhaps— with the efficiency of his machine."

"Of course," Carol interrupted, "I listened to that recording while Butch and I waited here for you. The man makes no threats, but if he doesn't get the money from this country, I'll give you odds there are other nations who would pay him for such a weapon. That man holds all the cards, and even the deck is stacked in his favor."

"Stacked decks have been known to deal phony cards," Quinn reminded her. "What you say is true. I'm afraid this man will give another exhibition of his machine, and there will be further murders. Even if he gets his money, there is no indication he won't want more. We're dealing with a criminal, an especially lowdown rat, who should be exterminated and his method of mass murder turned over to the federal authorities."

"Yeah," Butch put in, "but how do we find a guy like that and stop him cold, huh?"

"We have one lead," Quinn said thoughtfully. "The man who was blown to pieces at the airport. Of course his identity can't be traced. We may be able to learn where he came from. He was injured, his left foot twisted. He was covered with dirt and dust, indicating he'd fallen.

"Now a man, injured like that, obviously couldn't travel very far. He took a taxi at a certain address which I'll give you. Carol, you and Butch go there and look for an empty house with ceilings that are falling down."

"Are y o u clairvoyant?" Carol smiled.

QUINN held one of her hands and patted it gently. There was something more than friendship between them.

"Hardly, darling. I managed to scrape the instep and sole of the shoe blown off last night's victim. He had been walking, for some time, on a floor covered with small particles of plaster—old plaster, too. Therefore, I assume the house or building he was in, must be falling apart.

"Even an unkempt housewife would clean up debris like that. Call back when you have located the place. Oh yes—there were particles of sand adhering to the instep also. They covered the bits of plaster, indicating that the man must have walked on sand last. Therefore, also look for a sandy area outside this house."

"And you, Tony?" Carol asked as she arose. "Will we be apt to see the Black Bat prowling about?'"

"Not yet—unless something really breaks. I've got to get the hack driver I told you about out of police custody. It shouldn't take long, and I especially want a ride in his cab. Silk will be waiting for your call. If you find anything, I'll be along as quickly as possible. Just watch your step and remember we are not fighting a bunch of beetle-browed thugs. Good luck."

Carol and Butch made their way along the tunnel, came out in the garden house and slipped from the estate through the side gate. Butch had a car parked not far away, and they drove directly to the region from which the hack driver had picked up his mysterious fare.

"You'd better stay in the car," Carol

told Butch. "I can duck a great deal faster and better than you. It takes half a house to conceal that torso of yours, and, anyway, nobody would suspect a girl."

"Suppose you don't come back," Butch said disconsolately.

"Then you can start tearing those houses down. I'll be in one of them. Park around the corner and keep an eye out for trouble. I won't be long —I hope."

Carol swiftly located three deserted apartment buildings. She went down the alley between the first two and used a small pencil flash sparingly. She looked for any signs of a man having fallen, and for sand which he'd picked up as he walked through it.

There were none, but in the next alley she did find a spot where sand had been dumped. Encouraged by this, she entered one of the two buildings whose side walls faced this alley. The doors were not locked so she was able to steal inside quietly. She examined one room after another, paying particular attention to the ceilings and floors. There was no plaster strewn about—in fact, the ceilings seemed remarkably well preserved in comparison to the rest of the place.

She visited the other building. The first floor, consisting of four apartments, gave her no clue, but on the second floor she found that the Black Bat's theory was correct. In one room of one apartment her feet scraped on tiny particles of plaster. There was something else which interested her —several pieces of rope which had been severed by a chunk of glass knocked from a broken window pane. She also picked up a twisted piece of cloth which might have been used as a gag.

THE mystery man who had been blown to bits had obviously been held prisoner in this old place. Therefore, he really had meant to give a warning, had been destroyed before he could accomplish his purpose.

Carol shivered. Had he been destroyed by some lethal device which could be turned on anybody—anything—and blast it off the face of the earth? The man would hardly have carried a bomb in his pocket—not after making an escape from this room.

She crept softly down the steps again. There were no signs of life in the building, but she was taking no chances. Her natural inclination was to search the whole place, but the Black Bat needed the information she'd acquired. Therefore, it was best that she forego any further investigation.

She was at the front door when the floor beneath her feet began to rumble, and, very faintly, from far above, came the monotonous sound of machinery. Carol gulped. Was it something which might be turned upon her?

She raced out of the place, turned north when she reached the sidewalk and kept going. Carol didn't see a big car turn the other corner just as she emerged from the place. She didn't see it stop and drop one man, who was well hidden by a turned down hat brim and a raised coat collar.

Carol was in the coupe beside Butch and rolling away fast when the mystery sedan turned down the street a moment too late to detect them.

At a convenient corner, Carol phoned Silk and reported her findings. Silk told her to drive back to the house, where Butch could pick up the Black Bat. They met, not far from the garden gate. Tony Quinn was now garbed in black. He wore a big hat of the same color, turned down to hide the scars around his eyes. They were a dead giveaway, but it was impossible for the Black Bat to ride around wearing his hood and cape.

"Be careful," Carol warned him. "I distinctly heard machinery moving—sort of a whining sound. I'll stay in the lab until you return.

Butch drove off with the Black Bat beside him. They didn't speak much during the fairly long ride down and across town. The Black Bat was busy checking the two automatics which lay on his lap now.

"Had to squeeze time," he told Butch. "Only got back five minutes before you arrived. I went to Headquarters in a taxi and rescued Steve Cobb. Incidentally, I knew his cab was parked back of Headquarters, and I made him drive me home."

"Sure," Butch grunted. "That's the only fee you'll get out of them birds."

"You're wrong," the Black Bat chuckled. "I even forced the meter fare on Steve when he didn't want to take it, because I got my money's worth out of that ride. In the cab I found several hand marks and fingerprints.

"Fortunately, I could see them very well in the dark. The police dusted the interior for prints, but missed these apparently because the murdered man grabbed at the back of the seat and smeared the compartment below the rear window with something that looks to me like ink."

"But what was he doin' with ink on his hands?" Butch wanted to know.

"I'm not sure—yet. Better pull down this street. It runs directly behind the one on which those empty apartment houses are situated. Stay with the car, Butch. If anything happens, use your own judgment.

If I don't return, tip off Commissioner Warner about this place."

THE Black Bat got out, slipped across the sidewalk and faded from sight in the darkness of an alley. He ran lightly along this, hopping blithely over debris that would have tripped a man equipped only with average sight. Nothing remained hidden to the Black Bat's super-sensitive eyes.

He reached a high fence and scaled it with ease. Dropping lightly to the other side, he crouched for a moment while he drew on the black hood and donned the odd cape. Guns ready, he stole toward the house which Carol had indicated was the one in which the dead man had been a prisoner.

There was a rear entrance, and he selected this as the best means of getting in unobtrusively. A moment later he found himself in a dismal, damp-smelling hallway. Whatever rumbling sound Carol had heard was gone now. A deathly silence held sway.

Cautiously, the Black Bat moved to the front of the house. He examined several rooms on the first floor, and when he entered the one furthest down the hall, he sidestepped slightly so he'd be out of the way of the door.

Someone was peering through the window. The Black Bat could see the man's features in prominent detail. He had a wide face, closely clipped
[*Turn page*]

blonde hair and a bull neck. His nose was flattened against the window pane as he tried to see into the pitch dark room.

Then, suddenly, the man vanished. The Black Bat didn't pursue him. He had too much of a start and, in addition, the contents of this house might prove more interesting.

On the second floor, he found the room which Carol had described, saw the severed ropes, the broken glass. Part of the painted wall was smeared with a black substance, like ink. The noise of machinery had come from above, according to Carol, so the Black Bat stole up the stairway on rubber soles. Both guns were in his hands, and his extremely sensitive hearing was on the alert for the slightest sound.

The ceilings, even in the prison room, were in good shape. Therefore, the particles of plaster must have been shaken loose by something like machinery. It jibed.

On the top floor, the Black Bat found a closed door. He stowed one gun away, turned the doorknob slowly and gave the door a hard shove. Something seemed to bar its path for a bare instant. Two things happened simultaneously then. The door gave, and the Black Bat saw a room containing what seemed to be a complete printing press, large enough to print a newspaper, though not on the same big scale as a metropolitan daily.

And there was a tremendous explosion somewhere downstairs. This time the ceilings gave up under the punishment. One whole section fell, hitting the Black Bat's shoulder, and sent him flat on the floor. More plaster fell, and the sinister crackle of flames were evident to his ears.

He got up, massaged his shoulder and ran into the hallway. From up the stairwell came a tower of livid flame. Rooms on the same floor with him, were burning furiously.

Was this some more of the super-crook's work with his invention?

There was no time to puzzle it out. The Black Bat retired into the room with the printing press. One side of the heavy machine had gone through the floor. In about ten minutes the fire would eat away the rest of the supports and the Black Bat would be lucky if he didn't crash into the cellar with the big machine.

CHAPTER V

Murder Advertises

HEEDLESS of his danger for the moment, the Black Bat scooped up the blank piece of paper and a rubber roller. He placed the paper upon the type already set up and used the roller to get a good impression. Without pausing to read the words, he folded the paper and put it into his pocket. His next move was to escape. He dashed into the hallway again, drew back hastily into the press room. It was the only room in the whole building that wasn't burning furiously.

He raised the window and looked out. He was five stories from the ground, no fire escape was in sight and nothing but sheer space was between him and the bottom of the alley. His eyes penetrated the crimson glow of the fire and saw a heavy cable burning rapidly. He knew then that this press was run from electricity, tapped from another building. The cable might have offered a way out, but it was already too late. Even as he watched, the cable parted and fell with a shower of sparks.

Sirens were screaming raucously. The fire apparatus was here already. The Black Bat groaned. It meant rescue—yes—but at what a price! He'd be exposed as Tony Quinn, supposedly blind attorney. The Black Bat's career would come to an immediate end because, if Captain McGrath didn't arrest him, crooks would ferret him out, and their guns would silence the deadliest enemy they had ever encountered.

He ducked back quickly. They'd managed to squeeze one of the fire trucks down the alley between buildings. The aerial ladder was already being raised. A sudden blast of heat made the Black Bat swerve about. He covered his face quickly. The fire had reached the press room now and was eating through the dried wooden floor like so much paper. The floor gave a sickening lurch, and another section of the heavy press crashed through it.

Something hit the wall just outside the window. The Black Bat saw the top of a ladder, saw it shake slightly under the weight of a climbing man. He made up his mind swiftly then and drew back against the wall. The room was filled with smoke already and within the next five minutes the whole building would cave in. The Black Bat had to fight time, and he possessed no weapons for such a battle.

A fireman stuck his head through the window and flashed a torch into the gloom. Prone on the floor, he saw a figure stretched out. The fireman climbed in, tested the sagging floor gingerly and then bent down to pick up the victim.

A fist lashed out, and the fireman went to sleep, painlessly and quickly. The Black Bat scrambled up, dragged the fireman close to the wall and stripped him of his big peaked hat, rubber coat, boots and asbestos gloves. Then the Black Bat rolled up his hood and cape, stuffed them in an especially created pocket under his coat and picked up the fireman. He climbed onto the ladder, waved a hand to those below and went down a couple of rungs until he was able to slide the real fireman's limp form off the window sill where he'd draped it temporarily.

He went, down the ladder fast prayed the big hat would hide his features. Then, on inspiration, he stopped as if to rest, but in reality he stretched out one hand and rubbed it against a burned section of the window sill on the third floor. Then he rubbed his face and smudged it enough to make identification practically impossible.

WILLING arms reached up to help him, but the Black Bat clung to his unconscious victim, stepped down off the truck and moved onto the street where he saw a fire department ambulance waiting. In a city the size of Manhattan, fire department members hardly were apt to recognize every fireman they came across, so the Black Bat felt safe in presenting his victim for treatment.

"Passed out from smoke, I guess," he told the doctor. "I'm okay myself. Be seeing you."

He walked back toward the alley, but stopped abruptly because a small crowd had assembled, and someone was shouting astounding news.

"The Black Bat is in there! I saw him with my own eyes! He wore a cape like wings and a hood. I am not mistaken, I tell you. Ach, you do not believe me. I am Kurt Miller. I own this property. I live two doors down the street. It was the Black Bat the fireman carried to the ambulance!"

Two radio cops decided to investigate and the Black Bat realized this was certainly no place to tarry. He managed to get a look at the face of the man who called himself Kurt Miller. It was the face which had been pressed against the first floor window of this burning building as the Black Bat had searched it. The man owned this property, and he lived nearby. Such a person actually cried out for an investigation, and the right time to do it was now.

Slipping down the alley, still clad as a fireman, the Black Bat managed to fade into the darkness beyond the range of the blaze. He stripped off the fireman's regalia and quickly donned the Black Bat's outfit. Then he crossed yards until he came to the house described by Kurt Miller as his residence.

There were no lights in the place, a two-story frame structure, indicating that Miller either lived alone or his family was away. The Black Bat crept up to the rear door, examined the cheap lock and had it open with a master key in two seconds. He closed and locked it behind him, walked into the middle of the kitchen floor and stood there, listening.

Chairs and other furniture offered no handicaps in the darkness for he could see them plainly. The kitchen presented glowing evidence that Miller was a single man and without servants, because the sink was stacked high with dishes and dirt had been carelessly swept into a corner.

Passing through the dining room, equally filthy, the Black Bat reached a rather spacious living room. His eyes darted around the place. It was just an average room. Then those uncanny eyes stopped, riveted on the bare floor beyond the rug.

There were numerous scratches on the floor, as if someone had squatted down in front of an ordinary oak cabinet. It had a door equipped with a rather good lock. This fell quickly before the Black Bat's prowess. Opening the door, he stared at the surface of a modern, expensive safe.

Getting beyond that glistening combination dial was past the Black Bat's capabilities, but he had an idea it might be worked. The contents should prove very interesting if Miller were involved in this business of destruction.

THERE was a mirror hanging directly above the cabinet. The Black Bat tilted this at an angle so that it would reflect the dial to anyone hidden behind a big, overstuffed chair in the corner. Then he moved the wooden door to within an inch of being shut. He walked about the room and very carefully changed the position of several articles.

On the mantelpiece, he gave a cheap clock a shove that made it almost face the wall. He disarranged a faded lace table covering, moved a chair about and left the general impression that the room had been searched and the intruder had done his best to rearrange things so there would be no hint he'd been there.

Then the Black Bat retired to the corner, concealed by the chair. He crouched behind it, looked up in the mirror and nodded with satisfaction. While waiting, he rummaged in his pocket and found the paper on which he'd taken an impression from the set-up type on the printing press. There, in utter darkness, his eyes read big headlines and smaller type beneath. It was a front page of a popular daily tabloid, faked cleverly so that it could be wrapped around a real copy of the paper and disposed of along the streets of the city.

To all appearances the front page carried a letter from the man who now signed his missive in a sarcastic vein. The printed signature read "THE TWENTY MILLION DOLLAR PATRIOT."

The screaming announcement ran: *"PAY THE TWENTY MILLION."*

"PAY THE TWENTY MILLION"
"Taxpayers—twenty million dollars represents the cost of a few destroyers of moderate tonnage. Or twenty odd big bombers. What good are these when an instrument I have perfected will blast them from the sky or the ocean in half a minute. Notify your congressman to approve a measure to pay this money. Wait for another sample of what my machine can do."

The Black Bat heard a key being thrust into the front door lock. He put the paper away and drew a gun. The man who called himself Kurt Miller barged into the room, anger showing on his broad features. He saw the disarranged lace runner first, then the position of the clock.

With a cry of horror, he sprang toward the concealed safe. He moaned when he saw the wooden door ajar. He squatted, and his shoes ground into the wood as he did so, leaving more of those tell-tale marks. Fat fingers began to turn the dial, and the Black Bat's eyes transferred the reflected combination to his brain.

The safe door swung open to reveal the interior packed with documents and rolled maps. Miller practically collapsed when he saw everything was intact. He quickly closed the door and spun the combination. Then he went to a table, opened the drawer and extracted an ugly looking revolver. Armed with this, he headed for the steps to the second floor.

THE Black Bat moved into action immediately. He had the safe open before Miller had inspected his first upstairs room. He unfolded one of the maps and gasped. It was a scale drawing of an important bridge, giving in minute detail every approach. Others were similarly well-done documents, invaluable in the hands of a spy.

From calculations on the side of the maps, it was clear they'd been drawn for use in air raid attacks. Other papers were equally sensational in content. And, from addressed letters that had been delivered by hand, he learned that Miller's right name was Muller. He was certain the man was a spy.

Recalling that the kitchen stove was heated by oil, the Black Bat crept to the rear of the house. Miller still was busy exploring the second floor. If he came down, he'd run into an unpleasant surprise, but the Black Bat hoped he wouldn't because there was no time to waste now.

There was a can of fuel oil in the kitchen. The Black Bat filled a five-gallon saucepan with it, carried it to the safe and deliberately soaked those valuable documents with the inflam-

McGRATH

mable stuff. Then he struck a match, as silently as possible, dropped it into the safe and saw flames leap up. There was no danger of the fire spreading, but those papers would be destroyed if the fire was allowed to burn three or four minutes.

He stood erect, reached into his pocket and took out a flat metal case. From it he extracted a sticker, cut in the outlines of a bat in full flight. He pasted this on the wall above the safe, stepped to a window and raised it silently.

As he backed away in the darkness, he heard Miller's first anguished howl and saw him trying to put out the fire. The wail was cut off and turned into a string of Teutonic oaths when Miller saw the Black Bat's brand on the wall. He ran to the open window, leveled his gun, but spied no target at which to shoot. The Black Bat was quite invisible now.

Very soon afterwards, Butch was driving the coupe around the block for the twentieth time in accordance with standing orders. He felt heartsick because it appeared impossible for anyone to have survived the blaze which had destroyed the abandoned tenement house. Still, Butch was determined to keep driving all night if necessary.

He heard a curt whistle, and a big grin creased his face. Turning in toward the curb, he opened the door. A dark figure came skimming across the pavement and jumped into the car. Butch drove serenely away then.

CHAPTER VI

The Inventor's Return

IT was another meeting in Tony Quinn's laboratory. He had changed from the Black Bat's regalia into comfortable tweeds and a smoking jacket. His cane was propped in a corner near the secret door and everything was set for him to assume his pose of a blind man instantly should the occasion require such a move.

Quinn pointed to the crude impression he'd taken of the printing machine type.

"It's more than obvious that this 'Twenty Million Dollar Patriot'—as he calls himself—is playing on the fears of citizens. It's true that the instrument he claims to have perfected is worth the money.

"He gave away recordings first, and now he's probably got a staff of men out distributing these fake covers, wrapped around real newspapers. They'll hand out a few and then disappear. The news will spread around quickly, and regular newspaper editions will be compelled to carry the story. It's a neat way to get publicity that might otherwise be held back."

"But Tony," Carol asked, "how in the world does he expect to collect such a sum of money without giving away his identity?"

"I don't know—can't even guess," Quinn replied, "but what worries me far more is his threat to exhibit that lethal machine again. There's no telling when, where or how he'll do it, but it will be done in as spectacular a method as possible."

"This Miller chap you told us about," Silk broke in. "Maybe he's involved?"

"Undoubtedly," Quinn agreed, "but can you feature a German agent trying to sell such an invention to a potential enemy of his own nation? Miller is mixed up in it somehow, but he can't be the Patriot.

"Miller is probably as anxious to contact this unknown man as we are and make him an offer. That is what we must prevent. It's as important as running down the Patriot, and our clues are slender. One thing in our favor—the Patriot undoubtedly will dicker with anybody and raise the ante as he sees fit."

"You said our clues are slender," Carol spoke up. "Are there any at all, Tony?"

Quinn nodded.

"Yes—Viola King! Her father may have perfected this invention. A man like Joel King wouldn't take chances and have only one set of plans or formulae. It would be too risky. Therefore I think I'd better see Viola at once, before anybody else gets to her first. Carol, will you drive me there?"

They headed for the city line. Joel King maintained his residence and workshop about six miles outside the city in the suburbs of a smaller town. Quinn once more wore his black clothing and the concealing, big hat. He was worried.

"It's about that trap set for me in the tenement house," he said. "Miller owned the place, or so he insisted to the firemen. Yet I can't feature Miller setting it afire. The trap had been prepared for my entry."

Carol turned pale.

"You mean that awful instrument of death the Patriot says he has was turned on the building?"

"I'm not sure. There was a terrific explosion that should have blasted the whole place apart, but somehow didn't. It was meant to burn to the ground, too. Miller would have been far away, preparing an alibi if he set it. Therefore I can reach only one conclusion. You were seen entering or leaving the place.

"The crooks took alarm then, realized you'd probably report to someone and prepared themselves to exterminate whoever showed up. What makes it so difficult is the fact that you were seen and probably will be recognized again."

"I won't be taken off this case, if that's what you're hinting at," Carol said stoutly.

The Black Bat smiled.

"I know better than to ask such a thing. It does mean you'll have to work carefuly though for your own health. The men we combat are ruthless. They must be to kill off a dozen fliers as casually as an acrobat turns a flip-flop and then publicize a statement to the effect that they will show their strength again."

"I know," Carol braked the car and slid to the curb. "But I still refuse to be left out of it. Tony—in those days long ago, before the bandages were removed from your eyes—we made a pact. Remember?"

"Yes — every word. You were to work with me, share all the risks and none of the glory. Well, here we are. I'm going to interview Miss Viola King again. Perhaps she might confide more readily in the Black Bat than she did in Tony Quinn, attorney-at-law. Naturally you'll have to wait here."

Carol stowed the broad-brimmed hat away as he donned hood and cloak. Then the Black Bat became the night itself as he sped toward the comfortable little bungalow where Viola King lived.

It looked serene and peaceful as he approached, but suddenly the quiet was broken by the sound of a break-ing window. The Black Bat raced straight to the back door. It was closed, but not locked.

He flung it wide, and a gun blazed, but the Black Bat's eyes served him well. He saw a pugnacious looking thug, crouched and guarding the door, in time to leap aside and avoid sudden death. The Black Bat's gun roared an answer. The thug dropped flat and triggered again, but his target practically was invisible.

Then he saw what seemed to be a gigantic bird in full flight bearing down on him. He gave a howl of anguish and tried to crawl away. A gun muzzle raked the back of his head, and he went limp. Without pausing to examine the man, the Black Bat leaped across his unconscious form. He heard the front door slam shut, and as he sprinted toward it a woman's muffled scream stopped him cold. It came from one of the rooms down the hall.

HE WAS torn between two desires —to save Viola King, for it had been her voice calling for help, or to pursue the gunmen who had invaded her home. He flung the door wide, saw a car come to a squealing halt.

Three men piled into it. Two of them were so bundled up that he couldn't see their features. The third was a counterpart of the one he'd battered in the kitchen. The Black Bat's guns leveled and blazed. The car spurted off. He noticed that one of the two men enveloped in a coat was short and slight of build.

Those shots would attract attention even in this sparsely settled section of the town. The Black Bat hurried to answer the cries for help. He burst into a room and saw a man of about thirty-five, tossing and straining at ropes that bound him. Another man lay very quiet in a corner. Blood oozed from a scalp laceration.

The Black Bat looked for the girl, but couldn't see her. Then a muffled cry came from behind a closed door. He twisted the key in the lock and Viola King rushed out of a small clothes closet. She started toward the young man on the floor, but stopped in her tracks when she saw the grim outlines of the Black Bat. She uttered one more piercing yell and slumped to the floor.

The Black Bat carried her to a davenport and then went to the injured man. He was about forty-five, strong looking and dark featured. His pulse was strong, too. With nothing to worry about there, the Black Bat concentrated his attentions on the younger man. He cut him loose and stepped back quickly as the man crouched and got set to attack.

"Wait!" the Black Bat snapped. "I'm not one of those who harmed you. I'm the Black Bat!"

The young man straightened up, gaping at the weird figure.

"The Black Bat!" he said incredulously. "Yes, of course. I recognize the outfit. Viola—I thought you hurt her."

"She just fainted. Tell me—quickly now because I can't stay here long—what happened? Who were those men? Incidentally who are you and that man in the corner?"

"I'm Hank Standish. I'm an independent movie producer and I own several theatres. I'm going to marry Viola some day. That man over there is Jim Halton. He and Viola's father used to be in business together.

"The men who came? I didn't even see them. They sneaked in and pounced on us as one of them put out the lights. I'm sure I didn't recognize any one of them. Did you?"

"Out with it," the Black Bat snapped. "You're holding back. You think I may have recognized one of those thugs. Maybe I did, but I want the truth from you."

Hank Standish looked over at Viola. She was just a blur in the darkness, but she lay very quiet.

"I wouldn't want Viola to hear this.

I'm positive one of the men who came here was her father. They made me stand against the wall, near that broken window with my back toward them, but I knew what they were up to. One of them slid back a small panel and opened the wall safe over there beside the fireplace.

"Only an hour ago, Viola told me there was just one man who could do that—her father. She said the safe might contain his papers. She didn't even know the combination to that safe herself. I managed to knock a vase through that window, and then you came."

"Go see how Jim Halton is coming along," the Black Bat said. His sensitive ears heard a faint roaring sound in the distance—cops coming on a still alarm, without sirens. Hank Standish obeyed and kept talking.

"Halton seems okay. He's beginning to snap out of it. I think—hey —the cops. I—holy smoke, where *are* you? This business is getting too fast for me."

THE Black Bat silently had slipped away, pausing only to pick up the unconscious form of the crook he'd slugged. Fortunately the town wasn't big, and police protection none too thick. As the radio car pulled up in front of the house, the Black Bat was running slowly toward the spot where he'd stationed Carol.

He saw the car and breathed a little easier. His prisoner began to squirm and moan. The Black Bat paused long enough to send him back into a sounder slumber. Then he crossed the sidewalk, after making sure there were no late pedestrians about. He opened the car door and groaned.

Carol was gone!

He couldn't possibly look for her. The fact that the car was here, intact, was indication that she'd left it voluntarily. Perhaps she'd gone to investigate the shooting. He dumped his prisoner inside, climbed behind the wheel and drove away until he came to a dark section of the road where big trees with overhanging branches completely shrouded the car except to anyone who might pass very close to it.

He kept his eyes riveted on the spot where Carol had been parked, hoping aaginst hope that she'd return. When ten full minutes went by, he knew this wouldn't happen. It was, of course, possible that she had seen the car containing the gunmen roll away, and had followed it.

There had been a couple of cars parked on the street within easy reach if Carol needed one; and she would hardly have hesitated to commandeer a private car if she believed it necessary. Carol didn't obey orthodox rules any more than did the Black Bat. Naturally she would have left the coupe for the Black Bat to use.

If such were the case, it was probable that she would return to Tony Quinn's laboratory promptly. He drove in that direction, his prisoner limply lolling against him. The Black Bat had plans for his prisoner.

CHAPTER VII

No Time to Sing

AROL BALDWIN remained alert after the Black Bat left her. S o m e t i m e s t h i n g s happened very fast, and if he needed help, s h e wanted to be ready. Five minutes went by. Then she heard a single shot. Her blood froze. Had the Black Bat fallen into a trap?

Then she heard the flat cracks of his automatics. More shots answered. There were a few moments of silence followed by another fusilade from the Black Bat's guns. Then, on the street running parallel with the one on which she was parked, a car motor started up.

Carol already was eyeing a cheap sedan parked about a hundred feet up the road. Now she jumped out of the coupe and raced toward it. Without the slightest hesitation she got in, found the ignition key in the switch and started the motor. She drove to the next cross street, turned the corner and saw a heavy sedan flash by. There was a glint of guns and she knew this must contain the men wtih whom the Black Bat had exchanged shots.

She picked up the trail easily and held well back so that she wouldn't arouse suspicion. They headed toward the speedway and kept rolling at a moderate clip until they were close to the city line. Turning off, they followed another highway for about six miles and then cut into a narrow lane.

For the last four or five miles Carol had been aware that a car stuck rather close to her trail also, but she paid little attention to it for traffic was fairly heavy. Certainly those men in the first car could not have warned any others of their kind that they were being followed.

Suddenly the car in the rear spurted. Just as Carol made ready to turn into the lane, the rear car shot in front of her, braked fast and cut off any hope of escape.

Two men jumped out, each holding a gun. Carol's motor was stalled by the sudden stop. The two men parted and rushed for either side of the car. They yanked open the doors and guns covered Carol.

"Well I'll be—a dame!"

"What's the meaning of this?" Carol demanded hotly. "If it's a holdup, I haven't any money."

"Get in with her, Mike," one man said. "Take her to the clubhouse and be careful. I don't like the gleam in her eyes. I'll follow in our own bus."

Mike, the burlier of the two, climbed into the back seat and shoved the muzzle of his gun against Carol's neck.

"Get goin', lady," he snapped, "or maybe you'd rather I blasted your head off, huh? Don't give me any of that line about being' innocent either because we been on your tail ever since you started to follow our pal's, see?"

Carol repressed a shiver, managed to get the car started and followed that winding lane until she topped a rise and looked down upon a golf course. The season was over, but evidently good care was taken of the grounds all year around.

SHE followed the road until she rolled up beside the rear door of the big clubhouse. There she was ordered out. Mike seized her arm and forced her into the building.

A center room proved to be Carol's destination. There were no windows. Two additional men were waiting. One of them was about thirty, slender, snappily dressed and betrayed his egoism in a slender, highly-waxed mustache.

"Well, well," t h i s man regarded Carol critically, "what have we here? Mike—you didn't make a mistake and tail the wrong car, I hope?"

"No, he didn't," Carol shook off Mike's grasp. "I was following you. I did so because I saw you running out of Viola King's house after you robbed it, I suppose. I wanted to find a policeman and have him stop you, but I couldn't even see one."

"She's balmy, Gus," Mike offered caustically.

The slender crook, who seemed to be in charge—and answered to the name of Gus—wasn't so sure.

"If you're telling the truth, lady, then how come you didn't pick up one of the fifteen or twenty traffic cops we passed?"

"If I had, you'd have disappeared before I got through explaining to him," Carol said. "Viola is a friend of mine. You can't get away with this."

"We have so far," Gus scoffed. "Now listen—tell me the whole truth and you won't get hurt. You were watching Viola King's house. You knew the Black Bat was there. Maybe—say—you might even be the dame who came running out of the tenement house. I only had a glimpse of her, but she was built like you."

"I don't know what you're talking about," Carol insisted. "All I know is that you must be a bunch of burglars. I had someone else with me when I saw you come out of Viola's house. He got off to call the police. Maybe they're coming here right now. Maybe they followed—"

"She's nuts, Gus," Mike broke in again. "Nobody followed her except me. Like you said, we parked and waited in case you and the boys wanted to transfer to another bus. When you kept going, we got set to follow along, and then this dame takes up your trail—so we chased her."

"We'll find out quickly enough," said Gus. "Mike—take a look at the car she drove. Check the marker plates and go back to town. Find out who owns the car. Maybe, if we're lucky, you'll discover the bus is stolen.

"If so, this obstinate young woman is going to be found in what's left of it, and she'll be as wrecked as the car. Take one man with you and see if you can find out what happened to Wicks. He was guarding the back door when all the fireworks began. I hope the Black Bat gunned him out, for Wicks knows where we're hiding."

"I'll be back in a couple of hours," Mike said. "I know just how to find out if that car is swiped, and whether or not Wicks is in jail. Leave it to me."

GUS looked down at Carol, who had seated herself primly on the edge of a chair. Her eyes defied the glaring anger in his.

"If this is a set-up, lady, you'll be sorry," he threatened. "We rigged this clubhouse as a hideout for plenty of bucks. You could save yourself a lot of grief by talking, you know. How about it?"

"I'm a respectable housewife," Carol insisted. "I followed a lot of burglars here, and you won't get away. I'll see you all in the police station where you belong, and that's all I have to say."

"Suit yourself," Gus shrugged. "Get up and walk ahead of me—straight to that door. Go on, move."

Carol obeyed and found herself in a smaller room which seemed to be used as a depot for golfing supplies. Old bags, clubs and baskets full of used golf balls filled half the place. There was a heavy chair which Gus pushed into the midde of the floor.

"Sit down," he ordered, "and behave. Mike will return soon. If he backs up your story, maybe you won't get hurt. If he proves that you're lying, then I'll know you work for the Black Bat—and lady, that means quick curtains for you."

Two men took up posts on either side of her. Gus told them that if she escaped, they personally would go through what had beeen promised as Carol's finish. Then Gus went out, closing the door behind him.

Carol leaned back and eyed the room. There was a single light, hanging from a wire almost directly above her. She saw that the room was equipped with a skylight through which she could see stars and the reflection of a moon. The only door led into the larger room where Gus and the others were waiting. There were no windows. Escape seemed utterly impossible.

Not only that, but the Black Bat didn't have the slightest idea where she'd gone. Hope sank to a lower ebb in her heart, but she never damned herself for taking matters into her own hands. As an integral part of the Black Bat's organization, it was

He lifted the real fireman into willing arms
(Chapter V)

her job to take advantage of any opportunity to assist him. If the result meant death, she was willing. Her father had faced it—and lost, bravely. Carol was cut of the same cloth.

Mike would soon determine that she lied, return here and then the man called Gus would do his best to make her talk. That was a horrifying thought.

Her best bet was to look for a loophole by which she could trick these two men guarding her.

Carol glanced at the scowling men.

THE hip pocket of the man at her right bulged ominously. Carol leaned back in the chair, opened the small purse she carried and smiled very innocently when both guards tensed. She withdrew a compact, opened it and studied her face in the mirror.

She removed the powder puff, started to pat it on her nose, then dropped it.

The man with the bulging hip pocket bent down to retrieve it. Carol suddenly grabbed at the exposed gun butt.

She gave a hard tug at the weapon, and it came free. The second man punched at her head. Carol literally slid out of the chair to the floor, pivoted and brought up the muzzle of the gun.

The other thug was half crouched, swearing softly and ready to spring. Carol started to get up.

Unexpectedly the door opened and Gus, with Mike right behind him, was framed in the doorway. Carol started to turn and the thug on her left leaped and knocked the weapon spinning.

Gus walked swiftly up to her, grabbed one arm and hauled her up. Then he pushed her roughly into the chair.

"Just a nice peaceable housewife, are you? It takes a dame with brains to get the best of my boys—even those two dopes. What's more, Mike just got back and says the car you were driving was swiped from in front of a house on the street back of Viola King's place. All of which leaves you in an awful spot, lady. Well—do you talk or shall we try a few tricks that usually serve to loosen even a man's tongue?"

"Give me time to think." Carol brushed a hand across her face as if she were tired. "Five minutes. I-I can't make up my mind now. I . . ."

"Stay right in front of her, Mike," Gus ordered. "You two saps who let her snatch your gun—stand on either side of her. She'll have time to think all right. I've got things to do—take me ten or fifteen minutes—and when I get back you either talk, lady, or it's the finish. And if you're stalling for time to let the Black Bat get here—that's okay, too, because I'm stalling for the same reason. I want him to come, understand? He'll get here all right, but he won't ever leave —believe me."

GUS slammed the door on his way out. Mike slowly drew a gun and held it limply—just a suggestion that she'd die fast if she attempted to escape. A deathly quiet settled. Two or three minutes later it was broken by the croak of a bull frog. Carol shivered. Perhaps the marsh where he held sway would be the spot she'd inhabit from now on—if Gus changed his mind about wrecking her with the car she'd stolen.

Then Carol almost gasped aloud. The bull frog absolutely was insistent about it all. His croaks were frequent and loud. Carol relaxed completely and even Mike and his two men seemed to be overcome by the quiet. Mike yawned lustily, but in the middle of it he gave a strangled gasp.

Carol began singing—at the top of her voice.

She sounded like the happiest girl alive.

CHAPTER VIII

The Exploring Death

DRIVING straight back to his house, the Black Bat parked not far from the garden gate entrance and made certain his prisoner still was u n c o n s c i o u s. He pushed him far down in the seat so no passerby would see him and then glided like the night itself toward the gate.

Silk met him in the laboratory and the Black Bat ordered:

"Put on your simplest disguise and go to the car. Drive the mug inside it to a park, drag him out and let him recover. Then hide and watch him. He'll head straight back to whatever rat hole the rest of his kind frequent. Follow him—and whatever you do don't lose him—for Carol hasn't reported!"

Without a word, Silk opened a drawer and began to disguise himself.

"I believe Carol either has trailed those birds to their hideout and is watching them or they've captured her, Silk. This thug will lead you to her—so don't miss. If you find you are outnumbered, contact me here. If I'm not around, Butch will be; and I'll tell him how to reach me."

Silk changed his clothes to a cheap brown suit, and used his makeup kit. He no longer looked like the smooth, polished, ex-confidence m a n a n d servant. His face was uglier, his head no longer bald. He put a long barreled thirty-two automatic into a hip holster.

Slipping through the tunnel, across the estate and out the garden gate, Silk reached the coupe and found the thug still unconscious. In the park, Silk stopped at a dark, isolated spot and hauled the man out. He searched him first, but found nothing of conse-quence. Leaving the man sprawled out beneath a bush, Silk retired to hide behind a thick tree trunk. In the inky darkness he'd never be seen.

Minutes slipped by and Silk grew impatient. Like the Black Bat, he believed that Carol had been captured. Silk's lips were drawn into a thin, straight line. If she were dead—or injured—he meant to play a grisly song with his automatic.

Then the thug sat up slowly, rubbed his swollen chin and looked around. He got to his feet, swayed drunkenly and began to lumber toward the road. Silk reached the coupe and followed him at a discrete distance. This coupe was an old, rather badly used piece of junk on the surface, but there was a smooth, powerful motor under the hood. It could never be traced to the Black Bat and the motor couldn't be heard ten yards away when turning over slowly.

The thug clearly had no idea where he was, but lights beckoned him toward the edge of the park. Reaching an avenue fairly heavy with traffic, he stopped long enough to find out whether or not he'd been robbed. Finding money, he yelled at a passing cab and got in. Now Silk really had a job on his hands, for that cab rolled fast.

THEY headed across town to the elevated speedway on the West Side. Silk cut into the lane of swiftly moving traffic on the express highway, picked up the cab again and held a steady pace until the cab shot off the busy highway and headed into a state road. It followed this for several miles and then slowed. Silk allowed his coupe to coast off the road into the protection of the darkness around the shoulders. The thug got out of the cab, paid the driver and began to trudge along. The cab turned around and returned to the city.

Silk realized he was bound for some nearby hideout, so he followed on foot. Suddenly the crook disappeared up a side road. Once or twice he looked around, but Silk was a capable shadow and an indistinct shadow among shadows.

He followed the man almost to the clubhouse when he heard the whine of a motor car down the road, and dropped flat. The car pulled up at the rear entrance of the place and two men got out.

Rather faintly from somewhere above, Silk heard sounds of a brief scuffle. There was a moon and it gave light enough so he was enabled to see the partly open skylight. The noise came from there. Silk darted toward the building, tested the strength of a drain pipe and climbed it, easily and soundlessly. He squirmed across the room until he could peer through the skylight.

Carol was seated in a chair and being threatened by Gus. Silk heard the conversation, knew his time to act was limited and tried to determine how he could rescue Carol without exposing her to additional danger.

Crawling back, Silk slid down the drain pipe. He saw the vague outlines of a workshed about a hundred and fifty yards to the left. The small structure was locked, but the lock gave way readily to a short bit of steel which Silk was proficient at using. Inside, were the lawn mowers and equipment used to keep the course in a good state of repair. Silk found a coil of rope, slung this over one shoulder and stepped behind the supply shed. In his pocket he carried pliers equipped with wooden handles.

Now came the most ticklish part of his job. Silk had formulated a plan, but it was necessary that Carol know of it to carry out her end.

He had good inspiration when frogs in the swamp at the edge of the golf course croaked at the moon. Silk let out a loud croak. It sounded life-like. Then he set up croaking din, but there was method in his madness for, by a simple code, he signaled Carol to be ready and that escape would be effected through the skylight by means of a convenient rope.

He repeated this several times, jealous of the minutes that were wasted. Then Silk heard a clear, ringing voice. Carol was singing.

Silk followed the fringe of trees until he faced the back of the place. He waited a moment or two in order to make sure the crooks hadn't caught onto the meaning of those croaks and of Carol's singing. Then he reached the drain pipe and climbed it once more. Slithering across the roof top he took another look through the skylight. Silk would have liked this affair much better if the Black Bat were at his side.

THE electric light wires ran from a pole at the west side of the clubhouse to a point not a dozen feet from where Silk lay. In the room below, Gus had returned to investigate Carol's crazy singing. To motivate it, Carol just smiled a silly grin at him, kept humming and tapping her foot in time to the tune. Gus wrinkled his nose, turned and walked out again.

Silk was busy preparing a loop in one end of the rope. He got it set to drop quickly and then crept over to where the electric light wires were installed. He cut them with the wooden handled plier, heard shouts from the room below and the sound of running, blundering footsteps. He reached the rope and let it fall.

Instantly it grew taut. Silk, no longer cautious now, stood up, braced himself and pulled Carol up until she was able to grasp the skylight frame and haul herself to the roof with Silk's eager help.

In the room below, Gus and two other men practically were fighting among themselves to find Carol in the pitch darkness. Someone lit a match. A scraping sound on the roof brought all eyes ceilingward. Gus yelled a curse as he saw Carol's ankle disappear through the skylight. He whipped out a gun and fired blindly. His men also joined in the shooting.

BUTCH

Silk's gun was in his hand. He motioned Carol to run for it, leveled the automatic and fired twice. A scream of pain attested to his marksmanship. Silk took a long chance then. There was a bank, rising about eight feet behind the clubhouse and reaching a point almost level with the roof. He gave a running jump, cleared the space and landed lightly. He slid down the bank and found Carol waiting.

"We'll cut across the edge of the golf course," he told her. "Against the dark background of the trees we're less likely to be seen."

"Isn't—the Black Bat along?" Carol panted.

"No—I'm handling this job alone though I'll confess it looked too much for me ten minutes ago. Let's get started."

They ran quickly to the southwest corner of the course and then streaked due south, keeping well hidden in the shadows. No shots came from the clubhouse, no men poured out of it to take up the hunt. Just a grim, ominous silence held sway and Silk didn't like it. Mugs like the ones who had captured Carol didn't give up so easily—or if something did impel them to —they'd have streaked toward their getaway cars.

Silk looked over his shoulder and gave a grunt of amazement. From one of the windows in the clubhouse came a soft, brownish yellow ray of light. Not exactly a beam, but just a light with none too much candlepower. It kept moving slightly, like a searching finger.

Carol saw it too. 'What does it mean, Silk? Do you think. . . . ?"

"The invention those crooks may have? I don't know, Carol, but we've got to keep going. I . . ."

Suddenly a whole section of the earth—twenty feet in front of them, seemed to rise into the air. A terrific explosion accompanied this. Silk grabbed Carol and threw her flat on the ground. Dirt and stones thudded down upon their backs. When the fury subsided, Silk whispered words of encouragement to Carol and both of them arose and ran forward again.

Another explosion, this one even closer, hurled them off their feet. Silk grabbed Carol's hand.

"We'll take a chance and cut directly across the golf course. Perhaps they spotted us and are turning that infernal machine our way—using it more or less blindly in the hopes of blasting us into bits. They won't expect us to risk an open dash for safety. Let's go—and fast."

They covered about a quarter of the distance across the field when that brownish yellow light flickered again, moving slowly as if by a gunner finding his range. A dozen yards to their left the earth was blasted. Dirt cut into Silk's face. Half blinded, he stumbled on. Carol threw an arm around his waist and they kept going.

Two more gigantic explosions, dangerously close, impeded their progress and then Carol took a long chance. Guiding Silk, she veered toward the further end of the field. As she reached its protecting shadows, a whole section of the surrounding brush leaped into the air. Silk stumbled and fell.

CAROL dropped, covering the back of her head with her clasped hands. Big pieces of shattered wood fell around them. Silk groaned as a piece of rock landed on his left shoulder.

"Crawl," Carol urged. "Crawl, Silk. There's a big crater where that explosion took place. We can hide in it until you recover. This way—hold my hand tightly."

Silk followed Carol, sliding down into the depths of a shallow crater. Carol went to work then, with a piece of her dress torn from the hem. She cleaned out most of the dirt from Silk's eyes.

"If that's a sample of what they can do with their invention — it's worth five times twenty million dollars," Silk grunted. "That damned thing followed us around like a dog on the scent. In daylight we'd certainly have been blasted to bits. Wait until the Black Bat hears about this sample of what they can do."

"Silk," Carol said curtly, "they're leaving. Both cars — without headlights—but I can hear the motors and see them once in awhile. Perhaps they'll search the whole golf course to see whether or not they disposed of us."

But the two cars rolled rapidly to the road and disappeared. Both Carol and Silk held their breaths, listening to the fading sound of the motors.

"They won't come back," Silk said softly. "Those explosions must have been heard in the distance and when their source finally is traced, those crooks don't want to be around here. Of course they took that machine with them, but just to make sure, let's risk going back to the clubhouse for a look."

"Why not?" Carol answered. "If the machine and its operators are gone, we should be safe enough."

Nothing happened as they headed back to the clubhouse. Silk found the door wide open. Gun in hand, he motioned Carol to stand aside. Then he bolted through the door, prepared to answer shot for shot if this were an ambush. Silence greeted him. He drew his flashlight, sent the beam inquiring into dark corners and then called to Carol.

They searched the place rapidly until they reached the room whence the brownish yellow beam of light had originated. This proved to be a shower room. The floor was made of cement and—encased in the cement were four heavy bolts, like those used to hold machinery in place. That alone was their clue to the Patriot's death dealing device which had tried to ferret them out and destroy them.

"Nothing," Silk groaned. "We'd better get out of here ourselves now. The coupe is parked on the highway and those mugs won't have seen it.

Let's go—the quicker the Black Bat hears of this, the better."

"Yes," Carol agreed. "We can't waste a moment now—after actually having had the death machine directed at us. One thing though—I'd recognize any of those crooks again."

CHAPTER IX

Financier of Death

RELIEF flooding Tony Quinn's face at sight of them was a plain indication of how much he cared for these two aides of his. In the privacy of the hidden laboratory, Silk and Carol told him just what had occurred.

"That doggone light just kept sweeping the golf course like a searching finger," Silk said. "Then—I suppose—it picked us out and—blooey—we were in the middle of a blitzkrieg! I'm telling you, sir, it's the most ghastly thing I ever experienced."

"It must have been," Quinn said. "We know what we're up against now. Carol, that man you knew as Gus sent one of his men, named Mike, back to town in order to find out whether or not the car you'd appropriated was stolen. Was Mike pretty sure of himself when he got back?"

"He was positive, Tony. Not only about the car, but also the fact that some fellow crook named Wicks hadn't been locked up."

Quinn frowned. "That means the mob has contact at headquarters, somehow. I have ideas, but they are based only on suspicion so I won't voice them now. The bolts buried in the cement floor of the shower room indicate that the machine is large and apparently heavy. It also works under its own generated power. Silk proved that by cutting the electricity to the clubhouse. We've made a little progress at any rate. Now we all need rest. They won't try anything more tonight."

"What about that promised exhibition of their machine again?" Carol asked.

Quinn tapped the edge of the lab bench. "I've busied myself looking into possibilities. The Patriot, as he calls himself, has to give a really thorough exhibition of what his machine can do. Something highly effective and spectacular. Of course it's impossible to prophesy his next move; but I've learned that there is to be a test run of several torpedo craft on the Hudson tomorrow afternoon.

"Those boats are the fastest things on water and invaluable if anybody ever gets crazy enough to try an invasion of our country from the sea. The test hasn't received much publicity and could easily be watched from any of the various points along the course of the run. I think we'll go out there tomorrow and have a look around."

After Carol had departed and Silk returned to the house proper, Tony Quinn resumed his usual chair in front of the fireplace. His eyes were blind again, a cane rested betwen his knees and he puffed slowly on a well-heeled pipe full of fragrant tobacco.

His mind went over the details of the case. He put aside all thoughts of the death dealing device. That was just a machine and the destruction of it would mean little unless those men who knew its secret also were destroyed. The case was developing ramifications that coursed a winding path from Kurt Miller, a spy, all the way to pretty, little Viola King.

Quinn meant to question Viola's fiance at the first opportunity. He already had checked on Hank Standish and found that he was well known as a sportsman, a motion picture producer who worked independently, and something of a power in the entertainment world. He owned a number of small movie houses and seemed to be financially sound. Despite the fact that he was comparatively young, Standish had done rather well for himself.

He'd been roughly treated at Viola's house but not nearly as much as Jim Halton who claimed to be a partner of Viola's father. Was Halton trying to edge in on some claim to the stolen invention?

ADDED to this confusion of developments was the fact that Joel King apparently had returned to his own house, opened his own safe and removed certain revealing details of that lethal weapon he'd invented. Hank Standish had insisted Joel King was one of those men who had returned. But why then hadn't Carol or Silk seen him around the clubhouse? From their stories, the crooks fleeing by car hadn't stopped to discharge any passenger so Joel King must have traveled with them to the golf course.

Calmly, Quinn tried to sort the details into some kind of a workable theory. Joel King presumably had completed a death dealing weapon that worked, more than likely, by radio impulses. Yet the reputation which Joel King enjoyed counteracted the idea of his holding the machine for twenty million dollars ransom.

What was Kurt Miller's position in this mess? Was he a member of the mob—switching his patriotism from Germany and foregoing the placing of this great weapon into the hands of his fatherland's army because there were twenty million dollars involved? Or was he eager to lay hands on the device as the Black Bat?

There was grey dawn in the sky when Tony Quinn went to bed.

Silk awakened him five hours later.

"I'd have let you sleep longer, sir, but Miss Viola King just phoned and wants you to come to her house as soon as possible. Seems there is more trouble about her father."

Quinn sat up and rubbed his eyes. "Good—I meant to se her today anyhow. As Tony Quinn, of course—not the Black Bat. I want to find out more about what happened last night. How's breakfast coming along, Silk?"

"Very well. Fifteen minutes ought to be enough for a shower and shave. Miss Viola insisted that you were needed in a hurry, sir."

As Quinn ate breakfast, Silk read the headlines about the case of the Twenty Million Dollar Patriot. The explosions at the golf course had been investigated and it was inferred that they had been caused by some device similar to that used by the Patriot. Editorials were more or less evenly divided between condemning the Patriot and agreeing he should be paid —or just condemning him.

Then Silk gave a grunt of surprise.

"Wasn't there someone named James Halton at Miss Viola's home last night?"

"Yes—the Patriot's boys mussed him up rather well, too. Why, Silk?"

"Because this guy Halton happens to be a United States Representative and he's hinting rather openly that the twenty million should be paid at once to insure the government's getting the device as quickly as possible. Maintains we've gone all out to fight dictatorships—and stopped at practically nothing—so why should we hesitate to dicker with a crook and profiteer?"

"Is his picture in the paper?" Quinn said. "I thought it would be. Now just lay the paper on the table carelessly. When I get up, I'll have a quick look at it."

Quinn's blank eyes possessed life for a bare instant as he pushed back his chair. In that flash they glimpsed the portrait in the newspaper.

"That's Halton, all right." Quinn picked up his cane and tapped a path into the hallway. "Rather a perfect set-up for the Patriot, too. That is, if Halton is on his side. It doesn't take many congressmen to convince the others when it's a matter that more or less meets public opinion. Halton would be a good man for the Patriot to know."

"Why can't Halton be the Patriot?" Silk helped Quinn on with his coat. A car horn tooted outside. Silk looked through the window. "It's Steve Cobb, sir, with his taxi. I called him as you ordered, but I don't see why I couldn't drive you as usual."

QUINN put a friendly hand on Silk's shoulder. "Steve Cobb is all right and he inadvertently got into a mess. Nice chap, too. He insists on paying me while acting as my chauffeur. Tell you what—meet me at the office around twelve-thirty. And Silk—fill the hidden compartment of the sedan with the regular paraphernalia, will you?"

Silk sucked in a sharp breath. "You mean the Black Bat . . . ?"

"May go into action in broad daylight for a change," Quinn smiled. "It's a risky business, but I've an idea that the Patriot will try out his device on the torpedo boat tests on the Hudson. They're scheduled for two this afternoon and we'll want to study the situation first."

Steve Cobb was on the porch as Silk opened the door. Cobb took Quinn's arm and helped him down the steps. Quinn's cane tapped a rhythm as he moved along the sidewalk and into Cobb's taxi.

"Swell morning, sir," Cobb grinned. "Boy, wouldn't I feel lousy if they had me locked up in some old cell on a day like this. I would have been, too—if it wasn't for you. Where to, sir?"

"Let me see," Quinn stroked his chin. "There's a client on Malvin Street who wishes to see me. I think the address is something like number 602. Try that anyway."

Steve Cobb drove there in quick time, got out and rang the bell of Viola King's house. She opened the door, saw Quinn outside in the taxi and started to beckon him in. Quinn never moved a muscle and Viola turned slightly pink.

"Oh—I'd forgotten—he's blind."

"That's okay, lady." Cobb tipped his cap. "I'll bring him in. He just wasn't sure of the address—like he'd never been here before."

"Why—he never has," Viola said. "Please hurry."

Cobb helped Quinn out of the car and on the way up the path to Viola's home, Cobb asked whether or not he should wait.

"Yes," Quinn replied, "but it may take some time and I'll permit it only on one condition—that you allow me to pay the meter charge. Otherwise —it's no sale."

"Okay—sure, I ain't never refused dough yet, Mr. Quinn, but like I said, I owe you plenty."

"You owe me nothing, Steve. You've been very helpful and I appreciate it. I . . . ouch!"

Steve Cobb gulped. "Gosh, I forgot all about telling you where the step was. You okay now? Make it yourself?"

Quinn smiled. "My fault for not using the cane. I'm quite all right and—here comes Viola. Good morning."

Viola came down the steps and aided him into the house. There were three men seated in the living room and Quinn's apparently blank eyes never flickered with the surprise he felt.

One man was young Hank Standish—who might be expected to be around. Another was Jim Halton, congressman and alleged partner of Joel King. He wore a bandage around his head—a souvenir of last night's grim affair. The third man was known to Quinn, but only by sight and reputation. He was George Lockwood, a restaurateur known from coast to coast because of the chain of cafeterias he owned.

Quinn said to Viola, "You didn't ask me how I knew it was you on the porch. People usually wonder how I recognize them when I can't see them or they haven't spoken."

"You knew my footsteps," Viola said rather curtly. "Please sit down, Mr. Quinn. I'm in some rather awkward trouble. Oh—I'd forgotten. There are three people here. My fiance, Hank Standish, Mr. Halton and Mr. Lockwood."

"Congressman Halton?" Quinn stared blankly about six feet from the spot where Halton stood.

"Yes . . . yes, I'm that Mr. Halton," he said. I understand you are Miss Viola's attorney so I'll come right down to cases. For a long time I was associated with Viola's father as his secret backer. That is, I financed many of his experiments. Few panned out, but I kept providing the old fool with cash because I had faith in him.

"He was working on a device which would explode munitions, fuel tanks —even hydrogen gas if used in lighter-than-air craft. Such an invention would have profited this country tremendously. Well—I think Joel King perfected his invention and is now holding out for the fantastic sum of twenty million dollars."

"And you want half?" Quinn asked very gently.

The response came from Lockwood, not Halton. He laughed with his head back and his stomach shaking.

"That was the fastest answer I've ever heard pulled," he roared. "Halton—I'm afraid you've bitten off a worthy opponent in Mr. Quinn."

"I don't want a penny out of it— except what I actually put into the affair". Halton glared at Lockwood. "That's fair enough. But what is even more important is the fact that Joel King may dispose of this instrument to anyone who bids high enough. Oh, I thought him a harmless old codger until last night. See this bandage on my head . . . ?"

"He's blind," Lockwood whispered hoarsely. "How can he see?"

"Oh—oh, yes." Halton ceased patting the bandage. "Anyway there is a bandage on my head. Doctor had to take three stitches. Last night I came here, peaceably and willing to be convinced my suspicions were in error. Viola insisted her father simply had disappeared and she didn't know where he was. Just about the time she had me convinced, four men entered the house. They were all well muffled with scarfs and coat collars and each one had a gun. When I remonstrated with one of them I was hit over the head with a gun butt."

"What in the world did four gunmen want here—with Viola King?" Quinn asked sharply.

"I'll tell you," Halton cut off Viola's effort to speak first. "Just before I passed out, I had a look at one of those men. It was Joel King —I swear it. He came here to open a wall safe and remove from it all the papers and drawings he had made in connection with his death machine. You know what happened to those bombers. They were blown to smithereens. Joel King did that."

"But if Joel King wanted his own papers, why didn't he openly return for them?" Quinn asked. "That would have been the most natural thing to do."

"Because he knows the police and the G-Men are after him. Because he knows that I'd turn him over in half a second if I ever laid hands on him. That man has changed from a harmless, crackpot inventor into the greatest menace this or any other nation has ever faced. With his death machine he can blast anything, anywhere, at will."

LOCKWOOD put in soothingly: "Oh come now. "You're getting all wrought up about this, Halton. You were the only person out of three who recognized Joel King. Perhaps you were mistaken. Certainly his own daughter and her young man would know Joel King if he appeared. They were here, too, you remember."

"I know what I saw," Halton insisted. "And I admit getting wrought up. Who wouldn't—with this maniac running around loose? I know what Joel King can do because he told me his hopes. That's why I have already started things humming to arrange a payment to the man. We'll pay him, get the device and then hunt him down like the rat he is."

Quinn wasn't listening too intently as Halton raged. He was thinking of Hank Standish, who had informed the Black Bat that he recognized Joel King the night before and now indicated he hadn't recognized anyone.

Lockwood arose and signaled Halton to remain seated. He approached Quinn and looked at him.

"Halton is in a peculiar position. He assisted in promoting this death dealing device which Joel apparently invented. He's a regular financier of death.

"Now Halton is betwixt and between. As a congressman he must decide whether or not to pay this crazy demand for something he helped to create. What Halton wants from all of you is complete secrecy about this. He intends to ask that the sum be paid.

"If the newspapers d i s c o v e r his true position — well, use your own

---

Hijacked Payrolls, Looted Warehouses and a Flood of Counterfeit Money Draw Tony Quinn into the Toughest Mystery Maze of His Career in

THE SHADOW OF EVIL

A Complete Book-Length Mystery Novel
Featuring THE BLACK BAT

By G. WAYMAN JONES
Coming Next Issue

Had he been warned to kep quiet or was he just protecting the girl he loved? And Viola—just a bit cleverer than she pretended. Few people guess that a blind man can distinguish people by their footsteps, yet she'd caught on instantly. Rather different from the weeping, heart-broken girl who'd been in his office. Right now her eyes were flashing, red hot sparks of anger.

Quinn stared in space. "What should I do about this?" he asked. "If you're not after Joel King's property to get back the money he borrowed from you, I can't see where I fit in."

judgment. Halton is all right—perfectly honest and sincere. I'm buying out his brokerage house because he is patriotic enough to sacrifice every line of work to devote all his time to defense duties in Washington."

"I see," Quinn said slowly. "It does place Mr. Halton in a peculiar position. So far as I'm concerned, you have my word not to speak. I'm sure the others also will respect your position."

"By the way," Quinn continued, "just what is your interest in this case? If I seem rude in asking, please remember that Viola King is my client and I must protect her."

Lockwood's smile faded quickly. "Why I—I'm practically an associate of Congressman Halton. We—a—intend to carry out some important business. Now I can't let him get sewed up in something like this without trying to help him."

"I asked Lockwood to come," Halton said hotly. "Insisted on it in fact. Lockwood is a clever man—and one of my very best friends. He has a perfect right to be here."

Halton grabbed his hat, glared at Viola and Hank Standish and then stalked out. Lockwood smiled, bowed and followed him. Viola remained stony-faced. She turned on her heel and walked briskly out of the room.

"Am I alone?" Quinn asked somewhat petulantly.

"No sir—I'm here—Hank Standish. Say, Halton is a pretty temperamental fellow, isn't he?"

"Oh—yes, of course. Mr. Standish you were also here last night when those men, described by Halton, invaded the house. Were they unnecessarily rough with Mr. Halton—with you—or Viola?"

"One of them just walked up to Halton and conked him one and—I owe that mug a favor now because that's what I've felt like doing all along. Halton says he owns half of everything Joel King left. He has notes and papers, but Viola says her father never told her anything about signing over his inventions. Sure they got tough with Halton and me too. They tied me up."

"And Viola?"

"We-ell—they just pushed her into a closet and locked the door. Firm about it, but they didn't harm her."

"And you are certain Joel King was not one of those four men? The fact that Halton was injured shows somebody in that quartet hated him. You were more or less neutral to that party and Viola was treated gently. Doesn't that indicate Joel King?"

"Maybe it does," Standish snapped, "but he wasn't one of them. I got eyes. I can see."

And a tongue which could also lie, Quinn thought. He arose, moved his cane before him and almost tripped on a slightly elevated door sill. Standish sprang forward to steady him.

"I'm sorry," Standish said. "I didn't mean to get sore, but Halton was so insistent and Viola has suffered so much . . ."

"I understand," Quinn said. "Now, if you have nothing more to tell me, I think I'll get back to my office. Halton won't make any trouble immediately. His threats to use those demand notes were simply meant to intimidate you and Viola so news of his financial help to Viola's father wouldn't be made public."

Standish nodded. "Yeah—I guessed that after he started talking. Want to know what I think? Halton knows all about the invention. He wants to pay off this—this killer and then horn in on the profits."

Viola didn't appear again and Steve Cobb was running up the walk as Quinn reached the steps. Quinn went straight to his offices. On the way he tried to puzzle out a few things—especially where Halton was concerned. The man was certainly in an ideal position to put over this deal. He was one of the few persons that knew Joel King worked on such a device. He must also have known how close to perfection it was inasmuch as he financed the whole affair.

Now he could put pressure in the right places, induce the payment of an incredible sum of cash to this man who called himself the Patriot. Could Halton be the Patriot? And why did Standish lie and Viola cease her act of an innocent, coy young girl? In a more minor vein, he wondered what George Lockwood was doing with Halton.

True, as a friend and possible business associate, he did have a legitimate right to stick with Halton and do what he could to assist him—but was he remaining a bit too close? There was Kurt Miller to think about, too. The spy hadn't put in an appearance since the fire in his tenement. Kurt Miller was a man to beware of if Tony Quinn could read faces correctly. It was even possible that Miller might be the Patriot. Certainly he would be willing to dicker with the man for the purposes of getting that invention. This fact rather explained the reason why the Patriot so callously resorted to murder. He played two games—one with the United States authorities, the other with Miller and his Axis Powers. Perhaps he hoped to collect from the highest bidder—or even both of them?

CHAPTER X

Publicity for Murder

LIEUTENANT Commander Pierce, in charge of the torpedo tests, held the receiver of his telephone so hard his knuckles glistened starkly white.

A calm voice was giving him a dire warning:

"This is the Black Bat, Commander. You will recall that a man who calls himself the Patriot and claims to have exhibited the powers of a death-dealing device has promised further proof of his claims. He requires something very big—something that will stun the entire nation. I'm afraid your test runs today will offer him the best chance. Therefore I advise all caution."

Lieutenant Commander Pierce was torn between a desire to notify an aide and try to have this call checked, or to listen and accept the advice of this greatest of all crime fighters.

"I'm not accustomed to taking advice from someone I do not know," Pierce said, "but I do understand what you have in mind. I shall inspect the three craft most rigidly and maintain a constant guard over them. However, if this so-called Patriot does possess such a device, what good will searching the craft do?"

"Nevertheless—search them," the Black Bat insisted. "Be certain of anyone who comes in contact with the craft."

There was a click and the connection was cut off. Pierce hesitated a moment and then phoned Police Headquarters. Mention of the Black Bat's name brought him the instant and exclusive attention of Captain McGrath.

Pierce repeated what the Black Bat had told him. "Can the man really be trusted?" he asked. "Do you think I should take his word for this?"

"By all means," McGrath howled. "If the Black Bat even has a remote hunch, it always turns out the way he says. That guy doesn't fool, Commander. Take my guarantee for it."

McGrath hung up and then quickly raised the receiver again and told the switchboard operator to ring the home of Tony Quinn. McGrath received no answer. He tried Quinn's office and was told he'd left for the day. McGrath had a smug little smile on his face as he walked briskly toward Commissioner Warner's office.

The Black Bat had phoned Commander Pierce. Tony Quinn was neither at home nor in his office. Silk hadn't answered either. Therefore it was logical to assume, in the face of facts McGrath was certain of, that Tony Quinn and the Black Bat never could be in two different places at the same time and that Quinn had done the phoning. He opened Commissioner Warner's door, took several steps inside and then stopped cold.

Tony Quinn sat in a chair facing the Commissioner. Silk was parked near the window, a scowl on his face. Silk had little love for McGrath.

"You seem surprised — perhaps stunned would be the proper word,"

Warner said slowly. "What's wrong, Captain?"

"N-nothing—not a thing, sir. I—oh hello, Mr. Quinn. Just got here half a minute ago, didn't you?"

"Did I?" Quinn didn't turn his head. "Of course I can't see a clock, but I was under the impression I'd been here for . . ."

"At least half an hour," Warner put in curtly. "What's on your mind, McGrath?"

"Well—it seems the Black Bat just telephoned to the naval officer in charge of torpedo tests and says the Patriot may try to blow up some of those boats."

WARNER sat back slowly. "And you thought Quinn couldn't be here and make a call as the Black Bat at the same time, eh? You're getting stupider about this Black Bat phobia day by day. That's beside the point now. The Patriot would try a stunt like that. Think of the publicity! McGrath—select a picked squad of thirty men. Arm them with sub-machine guns and station them around the point where the tests are to be made. Cover the entire route on our side of the river.

"I'll contact Jersey Police and have them cover their side. Sorry, but I'm afraid I'll be busy. I—say—want to come along? There might be some fireworks to break up the monotony."

Quinn shook his head and McGrath, on the way out, hesitated to hear Quinn's final answer. McGrath was by no means satisfied about this. Quinn was and always would be the Black Bat in his estimation.

"No, Commissioner," Quinn said, "I'd only be in the way. Thanks for the invitation, but really. . ."

"Come along," Warner insisted. "Silk can go too and be your eyes— as he always is. McGrath—what in thunder are you hanging around for? Get busy!"

Warner abruptly left the office for a few moments. Silk arose and saun- tered over beside Tony Quinn. "Is there anything I can get you, sir? And do you really think we should go along?"

Silk brushed an imaginary bit of debris from Quinn's shoulder and leaned down as he did so. He spoke in a whisper this time.

"Who called in that warning, sir? Not you!"

"I don't know who did," Quinn an- swered and his lips hardly moved. "Certainly not Butch. I gave him no such orders. All I can figure out is that the Patriot did it. Why? To build up publicity—to get the full facts of this business smeared all over every newspaper. To train the people so they'll believe he should be paid off—and promptly. I . . ."

"Yes sir," Silk said aloud. "I'll be at your side every moment. Oh—it's Commissioner Warner back."

"We're all set," Warner jammed on his hat. "Take Quinn to my car out front, Silk. I'll be along in a mo- ment."

"Maybe," Silk offered when they were alone in front of Police Head- quarters, "it's just a stall to keep the cops and F.B.I. men concentrated at one point while the Patriot strikes in another."

"No—I doubt it," Quinn answered. "Destroying those torpedo boats would be an excellent method of get- ting necessary publicity. He issued a warning under the Black Bat's name because it would add to the interest of the case. Silk—we can't accom- pany the Commissioner in his car. What if something turns up? I in- tended to be on the scene as the Black Bat anyway. I'll insist I might be in the way and only agree to go if you drive me in my car. No use arousing McGrath's suspicions either—which we would do if we had to disappear suddenly when he was around.

"Warner's coming now," Silk said.

Quinn did some fast talking and convinced Warner he was right. Half an hour later they followed Warner's car through the carefully guarded gate leading into the Navy Station where the torpedo boats were parked.

"Holy Smokes," Quinn muttered. "Over there—talking to the Naval officer. Look, Silk—the taller man is George Lockwood and the other is my old friend, Jim Halton, partner of Joel King, instigator of a determination to pay off the Patriot. Drive over. Park close by them. I'd like to hear what they're talking about."

SILK brought the car to such a smooth halt that none of the three men, facing the torpedo boats now, heard it. Halton was talking.

"If you have completely searched all three craft, Commander Pierce, there seems little else we can do. It's a useless gesture, anyhow, because the instrument used to blow up those bombers required nothing planted on them. This device attacks energy stored up in such things as gasoline, explosives and the like."

Silk whispered, "I wasn't carrying any stored up energy when they set that damned yellow light in my direction. Nor Carol either. We'd used up even our physical energy getting away from the place. Yet those explosions and craters were not our imagination, believe me."

"Quiet." Quinn had his head cocked and those supersensitive ears of his listened to George Lockwood make a very worthy suggestion.

"If that's the case—about the stored up energy, I mean—then why carry loaded torpedoes. Of course you can't operate without fuel, and if the gas tanks exploded, your men would have a chance, but—if a loaded torpedo ever let go. . ."

Halton whistled softly. "Very good, Lockwood. I'm proud of you. Yes—those torpedoes must be removed and dummies substituted. Can you do that, Commander?"

"Of course — we'll weight the dummy torpedoes with lead shot to make their weight exactly that of the real ones. We're testing speed this time, you see, and must travel under average conditions. I'll see to it at once."

Quinn explained to Silk what he'd overheard. "Lockwood had a good idea there. I was going to suggest it myself, if I could find the proper loophole. All I hope is that somebody thinks of examining the dummy torpedoes."

"Tell me," Silk said slowly, "do you really think those crooks have to plant something in the object they're going to blow up?"

"Who knows, Silk? If we had the secret of the Patriot's machine, he'd be licked. The facts so far point to the idea that their device works independently and can pick out any target. Look—they're bringing the dummy torpedoes over."

"And there goes Lockwood, giving some more advice."

Quinn listened intently. "And good advice too—he wants them to open those torpedoes. It's time for us to be on our way. If Commissioner Warner wants to know why I won't stay —I'll tell him some excuse or other. Like wanting to have you describe the test to me from some point up the river where they travel full speed."

Silk turned the car around and drove to the gate. Quinn's eyes were looking blankly straight ahead, but he saw three uniformed sailors come out of a supply building. Each carried a box about a foot square.

"Ask the guard what those men are carrying," Quinn told Silk. "Do it without arousing any suspicion whatsoever."

Silk braked the car and two guards came over. Silk said, "If you see Commissioner Warner, tell him Mr. Quinn decided not to stay. This place is too busy for us to interfere. A minute ago I doggone near ran over three sailors. They were carrying a small box each and they walked like those boxes were full of eggs."

One guard laughed. "Oh, you mean those guys who came out of the supply house. They were carrying officially sealed speedometers to check the test run of those boats. I'll tell the Police Commissioner if I see him. The test will really look like something about two miles north of this point."

Silk drove through the gates and uttered a groan. "Oh-oh—here comes good old Captain McGrath and has he got an eagle eye on us. Do you think he'll try to follow us, sir?"

Quinn's head never moved as McGrath drove by, practically leaning three quarters of the way out of a window to see if anyone was with Quinn. He gave the blind attorney a sharp appraisal, but there was little satisfaction in that because Quinn never changed his expression nor the direction of his eyes.

CHAPTER XI

Murder Test

FIFTEEN minutes later Silk pulled up along a quiet spot overlooking the river. Below them the three torpedo boats would streak for a new record or—swift death. Everything possible to safeguard those aboard the craft had been done. Guards were posted, the boats searched thoroughly, no strangers allowed to come close by them.

Silk had chosen this place wisely for a clump of trees practically hid the car from the highway behind it. Tony Quinn quickly opened a hidden compartment in the rear of the car, took out a black suit of fine, heavy silk. He donned this and also put on a black shirt and tie. The Black Bat's hood and cape were handy. Two automatics went into his pockets and the Black Bat was ready for action.

He picked up a high powered telescope, got out of the car and made his way almost to the edge of the cliff overlooking the river. He used the telescope, studying the opposite shore intently. Within the next half hour those boats would come roaring up the river.

The Patriot had given warning that he'd attack—but where? Along the ten or fifteen mile course there were a thousand places which might hide him and his lethal apparatus. Patroling this section under such short notice practically was impossible. The test should have been called off; but the Navy never will be bulldozed.

The Black Bat gave an audible grunt. His telescope had spotted the brilliant reflection of sunlight upon highly polished glass. Someone, across the river, was watching through binoculars. He studied the area carefully through his own lens. Twice he caught a glimpse of men moving stealthily.

The Black Bat returned to the car and got in.

"Silk—get going. Take me over the bridge—two miles north of here. Then head south again until I tell you to stop. Go as fast as you dare. I've spotted them—on the other side of the river."

Silk speeded, then slowed and followed the line of traffic across the bridge at a leisurely pace because the bridge police were keeping it moving slowly. With a tweed jacket over his black suit and a robe covering his legs, Tony Quinn had his head turned slightly as if to sniff the river breeze sweeping over the bridge. In reality his eyes were riveted far down the river, looking for the first signs of spray from those racing torpedo boats. If he didn't reach the location of the killers in time men would die.

Then, to complicate matters, there was a slight accident up ahead and all west bound traffic was stalled. Silk fidgeted and squirmed. Tony Quinn had to hold himself in check. Ten minutes were wasted—minutes that might spell the difference between life and death.

They reached the other side, sought the narrow road running close to the river and Silk tore down it. Suddenly Quinn barked an order.

"Stop and shut off your motor. We're almost there and—the torpedo boats are coming. Hide the car, Silk. Find a hidden spot for yourself too and watch the river."

THE Black Bat donned his cape and hood, plunged into the brush bordering the road and vanished from sight. Silk concealed the car, got out and approached the steep cliff overlooking the water. He lay prone, glued Quinn's telescope to his eye and picked up the three speeding boats. They were half in and half out of the water, like racing dolphins. Behind them was a white fury of a wake.

Twice Silk heard cars pass on the road behind him—pass slowly as if patroling the area. This might do some good if the crooks attempted to get clear; but hidden—as they were —it would require a small army of police to comb this section.

Silk turned his attention to the boats again. They'd soon be about opposite the spot where the Black Bat had seen the sun's reflection against glass.

Then it happened. There was no warning, no preliminaries. All three boats suddenly disappeared, as if wiped off the river by a gigantic, invisible hand. Debris flew in all directions. There really wasn't much left to sink because the pieces were small and hardly identifiable.

Silk just closed his eyes and murmured a prayer for the men who had died to inflate the ego of a killer. The lethal device which Joel King had perfected must have worked like a charm.

The Black Bat was running egged on by the ever increasing roar of the powerful engines in those boats. Then came the explosion. The Black Bat's pace didn't falter. He knew just about where the murderer's lair was located and he meant to head off their escape if possible.

Someone, moving clumsily, reached a small, cleared space and kept running like mad. It was Kurt Miller— the spy. As he disappeared, two men suddenly burst through a heavy area of brush. They saw the tall, black clad figure with its cape outspread and looking like a great bird in the act of taking off. Both men reached for their guns. The Black Bat seemed to barely move his arms and then two automatics were blazing death. One crook fell flat on his face and never moved under his own volition again. The other gave a yelp of terror, turned and disappeared in the brush.

The Black Bat crashed after him, caught a glimpse of the man as he burst into a clearing and heard him shout an alarm. Bullets began to chop at the foliage and the Black Bat went into a nose dive.

He could see a wrecking car, just getting started. The cab was thicker than usual and he saw why. A narrow door still was open and through it protruded a squat, dull painted telescope-like affair. It was Joel King's lethal machine. Then the door was slammed shut by someone within and the truck raced away.

Six or eight men were left behind, but there were two other cars waiting and ready to whisk them to safety. The Black Bat lifted his guns, sighted them carefully and made certain the driver of one car wouldn't help the fiends escape. Then he concentrated on the other and repeated his performance.

Rolling over several times he escaped the fusillade of lead that tried to ferret him out. Five of the crooks were running toward him, separated and crouched like an attacking army of trained troops. The Black Bat wanted one of those cars so that he could take up the chase of the fake wrecking truck. The machine of sudden death was the paramount objective. These thugs meant little in comparison to that, but he had to clear a path through their ranks.

BOTH guns spat. One crook threw up his arms, staggered a few paces and then dropped to vanish in the tall grass. The others ducked out of sight. The Black Bat edged to the left, always drawing a little closer to the parked cars.

When he estimated that his chances of reaching one without injury were good, he plunged out of the brush and raced across the cleared space.

Bullets followed him and he fired over his shoulder a couple of times to discourage any attempts at real sharpshooting. Then he reached the nearest car, opened the door and pushed the dead driver aside. He slid behind the wheel, started the motor and rolled toward the second car. His guns blasted briefly at the tires when he was directly beside the vehicle. He doubted that they'd use this car in pursuit.

He reached the road, slowed and saw the tire marks of the wrecking truck. It had turned north. He stepped on it. Unless the wrecking truck was geared for high speed, he would be able to overtake it within the next ten or fifteen minutes. There were very few side roads and these were so bad that any driver, intent on escaping, would hardly have tried to negotiate them. Still, the Black Bat slowed up enough so he could have spotted fresh tracks.

He knew that somewhere, well behind him now, he must have flashed past the spot where Silk was hidden. Gripping the wheel, fighting the car over this rough road every moment, the Black Bat not only had to watch for the wrecking truck, but avoid any police patrols as well.

He was fairly certain that he'd gone beyond the end of the proposed test run for those torpedo boats and this area would hardly be patroled. However, the shots must have been heard and following so quickly on the destruction of the boats, all police must have recognized them as a clarion call for attention. Police cars would be following by this time.

Suddenly the road curved sharply to the left and the Black Bat found himself rolling downhill. The road no longer was hemmed in by trees and shrubs—just a vast, wide open area lay in front of him and—about a mile ahead was the wrecking car, racing at top speed.

The Black Bat laid a gun on the seat beside him, did everything but push the foot accelerator through the floor boards and gained on the truck. He realized that they'd try desperate means to keep the truck—and the secret it contained—out of his hands.

The truck left the road and began hurtling down a meadow toward the river. Just about the time the Black Bat began to worry if the killers were intent on driving the truck over the cliff and into the river, the driver changed course and bumped toward a summer cottage located about thirty feet from the edge of the cliff. Far below, the upper Hudson flowed like a sheet of silver in the late afternoon sunlight.

Very soon it would be dusk and then—darkness—wherein the Black Bat operated at top efficiency.

He turned into the meadow hardly relaxing his break-neck speed. Two men leaped out of the truck, but there must have been a third who drove because the truck rolled up to an attached garage and stopped. The men who had jumped out, opened the doors and the truck moved in. The doors closed and that was all there was to it.

The Black Bat stopped his car and tried to figure it all out. Three men in that cottage with the lethal instrument. Did they intend to defend themselves with it, blast anything and everything that tried to dislodge them?

That was the logical answer; yet the Black Bat showed no hesitation. He could reach the cottage in only one way—straight across the vast clearing. He'd run into gunfire or that deadly series of radio impulses and rays, whatever the machine operated on.

Flat on his belly, he wriggled a little closer, guns ready. He watched the windows and doors narrowly. If one of them opened, he'd fire instantly —give them no chance to get their murder machine into action. Nothing happened. Just a grim silence held sway; and the Black Bat didn't like it.

He sprinted closer to the cottage, reached its walls and flattened himself against the boards beside the rear entrance. There was no porch, just three small steps leading to the door. The Black Bat made a dive toward the door, grabbed the knob and twisted it. The door opened. No mass of hot lead came out to greet him, no brownish yellow flashes of a deadly ray were centered upon him. Just more of that grim, complete silence.

This had all the earmarks of a trap. Three men had entered this cottage. The only way they could have gotten out was by leaping from the cliff which was akin to suicide.

The Black Bat passed through the tiny kitchen, saw a door to the attached garage and headed that way. No matter what happened afterwards, if he could destroy the lethal machine, any sacrifice would be worthwhile. The truck was there. At the further end of the garage were a number of piled wooden boxes. The Black Bat paid no attention to them—he was far too intent on the wrecking car and what it must contain.

That was why he failed to see a pair of sharp, cruel eyes peering through an especially arranged peephole in the barricade of boxes. The Black Bat jumped aboard the truck, looked sharply for the hidden door he'd seen wide open as the truck moved off—and found it without much trouble. His sensitive fingers passed over the duco finish until they felt a hardly perceptible lump. Pushing this caused the narrow door to open.

THE Black Bat gave a hoarse groan of despair. The hidden compartment was empty. The truck must have been especially geared, travelled as fast or faster than his commandeered car and the lethal machine had been unloaded somewhere.

Suddenly the Black Bat whirled around, both guns at a ready angle. The three thugs who had been in the truck, were converging on him from three sides. The Black Bat didn't wait for an invitation to shoot. His guns opened up and two of the thugs jumped for protected places. The third aimed deliberately and squeezed the trigger with the Black Bat's head

[*Turn page*]

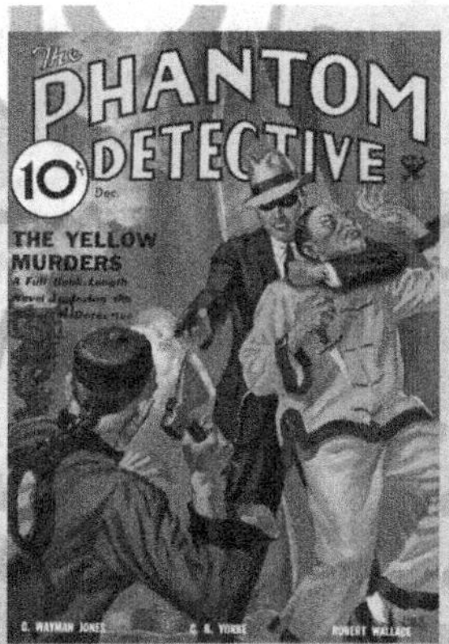

squarely in the sights. As the mechanism worked and a bullet went hurtling on its way, the Black Bat just let himself go completely limp and dropped like a sack of potatoes. One arm twisted around his body. Two gleaming eyes shone from the slits in his hood and—the gun in one hand barked. The thug went down, moaning.

The other two crooks took advantage of the Black Bat's preoccupation and fled through the cottage to the back door. They streaked out of it as if a dozen assorted devils were at their heels.

Silk—who had instantly taken up the chase—now was observing the cottage, from a point about a quarter of a mile away. He saw a car close to the house, but didn't know it was the one driven by the Black Bat.

Then the rear door erupted two men who pounded crazily across the ground. A third came catapulting out and then Silk saw the reason for their haste. From a spot directly opposite where he was hidden, came those brownish-yellow flashes of light.

The lethal machine!

Sirens were howling and brakes screeched. Police came rushing across the cleared space toward the cottage. Silk arose, yelling lustily and waving his hands. They couldn't identify him from that distance and even if they could—Silk would have done the same thing.

For some reason the crooks were intent on blowing that cottage into oblivion. Silk knew why about half a second later. The third man saw the police, veered sharply and ran straight toward the cliff. As he was almost opposite the house, a figure in black stood in plain view for a moment in the doorway. He had a gun in his hand and it roared.

At that instant everything vanished in a halo of smoke and destruction. Police were hurled flat by the concussion. Silk just sat down, very slowly, and closed his eyes.

The Black Bat had been in that cottage—he'd seen him and knew that the Black Bat was dead.

CHAPTER XII

Avenge the Black Bat

WHEN Captain McGrath and Commissioner Warner reached the scene half an hour later, a detective lieutenant, still covered with dirt from the explosion, told them what had happened.

"We first heard shots back there where the boats were blown up. We found a dead crook and heard car motors fading in the distance. We started a chase. It was slow work because we had to stop at the crossroads to see if they'd changed their course.

"Then we spotted this car—what's left of it is still down there near the crater. Anyway, just as we began to close in on the cottage, somebody stood up way over to the left and yelled like mad. We knew it was a warning of some kind. I looked all around and right over there—behind those trees, I saw a funny kind of a light. It was yellow—maybe brown.

"Anyway that's about all there was to it. Just before the explosion, some of my boys saw a guy come running out of the cottage. The Black Bat was inside, too, and started shooting at this mug."

McGrath turned pale. "Are you trying to tell us the Black Bat was blown up with the house?"

"That's it. He was right in the doorway, fighting to the last. The guy he shot at disappeared too—guess he was pretty close to the cottage and went up with the explosion."

Commissioner Warner turned away slowly. McGrath licked his lips, started to say something and then pivoted quickly. He gulped, walked up beside Warner and they looked at one another.

"I—guess that—finishes the case of —the Black Bat," McGrath said with a great sigh. "I always knew he'd go out like that—with both guns shooting at some louse who didn't deserve to live."

"Then why the devil aren't you happy about it?" Warner roared. "You've hunted the man until you were blue in the face."

"Well, I—I don't know. It seems like I—really lost a friend, Commissioner. Like you, maybe. I was pretty tough on Quinn at that, I guess."

"It wasn't Quinn who was blown up in that cottage," Warner snapped. "I left him at the Naval test grounds."

"Sure you did—and I saw him driving away. Look, Commissioner, I know it was Quinn. To prove it, all we have to do is go to his house and wait. He won't come back. Ten men saw him die. And that damned machine—look here, sir—I want an assignment like the one I had concerning the Black Bat. I want to run down the rats who killed him—if it takes the rest of my life."

"You'll have your chance," Warner said. "After what has happened, I don't think there'll be much opposition to paying off this leech who claims to be a Patriot. He'll get his money. If he doesn't double-cross us, we'll have that device he uses and then—then McGrath—go get him. Become another Black Bat if necessary. Throw all rules and regulations overboard. Shoot to kill if you must—do—anything. Oh, what's the use of talking? Our hands are tied. Everyone will be convinced of the efficiency of the Patriot's machine. We can't make a move until it is in the proper governmental hands."

McGrath blew his nose rather lustily. "Yes sir. But I'm getting busy at once. If I find anything, I'll lay low so as not to gum up any arrangements to contact the Patriot. Later on, I'll drift over to Quinn's house—just to verify things."

SILK made his way back to where Tony Quinn's car was hidden, got in and drove away, avoiding the police easily. He drove to town, rolled the car into the garage and walked slowly to the house. It was like a tomb when he entered. Silk's face was hard as granite, his eyes shining and cold with fury. He picked up the phone and made two calls.

Ten minutes later Butch was clumsily trying to comfort Carol.

"Look, Carol," he said, "he wouldn't want us to mope around. We gotta get on the trail of them rats right away. Ain't that the agreement—if any of us get—get—well just don't come back, the others must carry on."

Carol looked up. "Yes—of course, Butch. We can't waste a moment. Tony told us a great deal so we're not working in the dark. There are suspects to be watched. Silk—you take James Halton. To me, he seems very suspicious. I'll see to this Nazi spy—Kurt Miller. He simply can't be involved with the Patriot because he'd have disappeared with the lethal weapon long ago if he could get his hands on it. Therefore, I'll go see him, say I'm from the Patriot and let him make me an offer. If he has been approached before—which I rather think possible—he'll contact the Patriot or one of his men. Butch —you'll remain outside Miller's house and follow him if he leaves."

Silk was already at work donning a disguise. This one turned him into an apple cheeked, straw haired man ten years younger. An old, rather battered suit and hat finished the picture and Silk looked much like a farmer's son on a visit to the big city. Not too obviously so, but this disguise had tricked dozens of confidence men and they were among the most discerning crooks on earth. Silk was sure it would also trick the Patriot or any of his cohorts.

Carol was talking again, her voice steady, her mind clear and intent on one thing—vengeance!

"After I prepare the ground for Butch, I'll go see this Viola King. Tony wasn't quite satisfied with the manner in which she has been acting. It's hardly possible that she is involved unless her father voluntarily disappeared with his accursed invention."

"Hey," Butch looked up suddenly, "I just thought of something. Suppose McGrath comes snooping around?"

"Let him," Silk barked. "What difference does it make now? Our job is to concentrate on the man who is responsible for Tony's death."

Carol looked squarely at Silk. "You actually saw it, Silk? There's no doubt in your mind? None at all?"

"I'm sorry, Carol. He was in the doorway of that cottage, shooting like mad at one of the crooks. There couldn't have been any mistake and nobody—nothing—could have moved fast enough to get out of the way of the blast. Good luck with Miller. We'll meet here later on."

Silk jumped into the tunnel. Butch paced the floor with mincing steps that would have looked funny under ordinary circumstances. Carol had seen faces alight with hatred before but nothing to equal the look on Butch's features. His mighty hands kept working, as if there was an imaginary neck within their grasp.

CAROL drove her own car to the vicinity of Miller's home. She used a powder puff, rouge and lipstick rather lavishly before she got out.

"There's a deep doorway directly across the street from Miller's house," she told Butch. "Hide there. I'll go in and try to smoke him out. Tony knew all about him, but did nothing except destroy a lot of accumulated maps and things because he wanted to give Miller his head—let him lead the way to the Patriot. We're following Tony's plans, Butch, so don't muff this."

Carol walked boldly to the front door, rang the bell and when Miller thrust his lined face against a window, Carol signaled him covertly by exhibiting a piece of paper upon which was written one word *PATRIOT*.

Miller's eagerness to let her in gave away his whole attitude on this case. Getting that lethal device was Miller's one aim in life. He closed the door, snapped two locks and put a burglar chain in place. Then he faced Carol.

"You are from—him?"

"Yes. We are willing to sell to the highest bidder, as you probably know. You must be prepared to state a price, but first—can you raise the cash with the assets of your country frozen?"

"I can raise the money," Miller answered excitedly. "It would be worth it just to know the Black Bat is dead. I have heard. It was a clever job. I will also confess that I guessed your employer would blow up those new torpedo boats so—I was in a position to watch it all. Very well done. I am satisfied that your device is worth all the millions you ask."

"Good," Carol said, "but you must work fast. I am in no position to bargain with you, but—I take it you know who is."

Miller nodded eagerly. "Yes—of course. I have only been waiting for word to act. You shall go with me—eh?"

"No—I work outside the organization and take my orders direct from—the Patriot. You will proceed alone, *Herr* Muller. You see—I even know your right name."

Carol stepped aside while Miller unlocked the door again. She gave him a curt nod, walked out and hurried down the street to where her car was parked.

Miller watched her stride away, and a nasty grin spread over his wide face. He locked up, hurried to the telephone a n d d i a l e d a number. "This," he announced excitedly, "is Kurt Miller. A young woman was here—who said she was from the Patriot. That is a laugh. A spy—she was. It is a plan to have me lead the way and betray all of you. But I am too clever."

"What did the girl look like?" the man at the other end queried.

Miller gave a very good description and heard the other man curse.

"Yeah—I know her all right. Smart as a whip, too. Listen, Miller, here is what you do. They'll expect you to go somewhere and contact us. Go out in a big rush, walk directly to the small park half a dozen blocks north of your home. It's dark there. When you reach a pitch black spot, duck aside and leave the rest to me. She'll follow and it'll be the last time she works against us."

Miller agreed, hung up and hurried out of the house. Butch took up the chase, hanging way back, but keeping Miller in sight every moment. Miller made no attempt to see whether or not he was trailed, but just went briskly straight toward the park.

A S the German passed through a particularly dark portion, he heard a sibilant hiss and ducked behind a bush. Butch kept on coming, peering through the darkness for a glimpse of Miller.

Then two men hurtled out of the night toward him. Both held guns clubbed. Butch didn't move a muscle until the guns came up to finish him off. Then both his hands flew out, and when they fanned back in again each was grasping a thug. Their heads came together with a resounding crack and both dropped heavily.

But Butch, occupied with these two, was in no position to ward off the second attack from behind. Another pair leaped at him. Guns slashed down and Butch faltered under the impact. Still another man—suave, debonair Gus—stepped in close with a

blackjack upraised. This blow was effective. Butch sprawled on the grass.

The two thugs he'd knocked half senseless were helped to their feet. One looked down at the huge bulk of a man.

"I thought it was gonna be a dame," he grumbled. "That guy ain't human. I never felt fingers so strong—thought they was gonna bust my neck right in two."

"Yeah," the other victim of Butch's tactics stepped closer. His gun centered down at Butch's head. "And the best thing to do with an elephant like him is blast his brains out."

Gus knocked the gun aside. "You nit-wit. How do we know who he is? Cop, G-Man, or maybe a guy who worked for the Black Bat. We've got to find out. The way you mugs act shows why you're always going to be just mugs. There isn't a thimbleful of brains between you. Now get the car over here and toss this man mountain inside. We're going to the seashore."

"Okay," one of the thugs growled. "Plenty of water there to drown a gorilla like him. I'll get the car."

CHAPTER XIII

Hideout

S ILK KIRBY'S task proved much simpler. He went directly to Jim Halton's home, found it dark and used a picklock on the back door. Inside, h e refrained from turning on any light and used a flash with tape across the lens. Only a narrow ray of light showed. Halton's big desk seemed the most likely place to begin work and Silk picked the locks. They presented him with a mass of evidence—most of it rather astounding. First of all, Halton wasn't the wealthy man his reputation indicated.

In fact, he was all but penniless through some foolish investments. Lockwood really had bought out his brokerage agency and the money he'd paid also was gone. If finances meant anything, Halton was by far the most logical man to suspect.

Silk checked further, finding that Halton had disposed of several pieces of property. But the one easiest to sell, and for which he could have received the best price, was still in his name. A twenty thousand dollar home at the shore near Pelham. Its acreage and assessment indicated just how easily this could have been disposed of. Why? Silk wondered if the answer concerned a likely spot where the Patriot's men could hide and where that lethal instrument could be safely kept. At any rate the place warranted a visit.

Silk replaced everything exactly as he found it, gave the rest of the house a hasty examination and then returned to where his car was parked. He sat behind the wheel for a moment, reflecting just what the Black Bat would have done under the circumstances. His usual policy had been—when in doubt — attack. The answer to the problem would come much more swiftly then. Silk started driving toward the city line and Pelham, a few miles beyond it.

He knew that this would probably be the last case he or the others ever would handle. Without the Black Bat at the helm, continued fight against crime was hopeless. But—those who were responsible for the Black Bat's death were going to pay. Silk's mind was grimly made up on that score and he was sure Carol and Butch felt the same way.

Some of the details concerning the case had been locked up in the Black Bat's mind. To Silk, Jim Halton seemed the most logical man to suspect. He needed money, he knew about the invention of Joel King, he

was a congressman and in a position to press for payment of that huge sum of cash to the Patriot.

Lockwood's continued presence around the different scenes of the case also intrigued Silk. Lockwood was a pleasant gent—almost too genial and willing. Then Kurt Miller—Silk put him out of it. Miller's ambition was to acquire the lethal machine for himself. True, he'd probably go to any steps to insure getting the machine, but so far only the fine hand of the Patriot had shown in the crimes.

With a full description of the house and a mental picture of just where it was located, Silk had little trouble in finding Halton's big summer home. It had a private beach, fenced in, a big sprawling porch and many rooms. At least fifteen men could hide out here. On either side of it were two estates, much like Halton's; but both were closed because the weather would be unseasonable for weeks.

THERE were lights in Halton's house. Silk left the car, wished that he possessed the eyes through which the Black Bat had penetrated darkness so readily, and doggedly moved forward. He slipped a gun into his side coat pocket and kept his hand wrapped around the butt.

So far as Silk knew, Butch was trailing the spy and Carol was investigating Viola King further. He'd get no help from them if things went sour. Without the Black Bat it was clear that the whole business had been placed on a touch-and-go basis. Mistakes meant death.

Silk squatted behind the big garage and studied the house intently. The back door was closed and more than likely locked. All windows were down and so far as he could see, not an avenue for quiet entrance to the place existed. The best move was to lure one or more of the occupants out so they'd create an entrance for Silk. His brain clicked smoothly.

If lights should suddenly appear in either of the next door houses and the Patriot's gang was holed up in Halton's place — certainly someone would be sent to investigate. The presence of neighbors might interfere badly with their plans.

Silk cut across the estates, climbed the high wire fence and forced open the back door of the house to the south of Halton's place. In these big houses electricity was kept in service the year around so when he flicked a light switch, the room became bright. Silk lit the lights all over the first floor.

Then he hurried out of the place, went back over the fence and waited, his eyes glued on the back door of Halton's summer home. As he expected, the lights next door did arouse the curiosity of whoever lived at Halton's. The back door opened and a man came out. For a moment or two he stood revealed in the yellow light from the kitchen and Silk barely checked a sharp whistle of amazement.

This was Mike, whom Silk had last seen guarding Carol at the golf course clubhouse. It flatly confirmed his theory that the Patriot's gang did maintain their hideout here.

Mike was cautious but clumsy. He passed close by the spot where Silk was hidden and heard nothing until the butt end of a gun slammed against his skull. He went down without a murmur and Silk hurriedly divested the man of his tie, belt and shoe laces. He used these to bind him.

He put on Mike's coat, which was several sizes too big for Silk's slim frame and yet, in the darkness, lent the illusion that here was a big man. Mike's floppy brimmed felt hat went on Silk's head and he hoped that he could pass for Mike until he was close enough to silence anyone who might challenge his identity.

Head down, Silk moved back toward the house. Concealed under the copious folds of his borrowed coat, was a gun ready for action. The door opened as Silk stepped up on the porch and to his vast relief, only one man waited for him.

"Who was it, Mike?" this man asked. "You sure it ain't Cops or G-Men. . . . ?"

The door guard's speaking facilities were abruptly cut off by a short, hard punch flush on the jaw. As he fell, Silk caught him, eased the man's bulk into a chair and slugged him once more.

GUN exposed in his hand now, Silk moved softly toward a butler's pantry, stepped into it and peered through a circular window set in the door. The dining room just beyond was empty, but he could hear voices, apparently issuing from a room across the reception hall.

Silk pushed the swinging door open, slid through and with his back against the wall, sidestepped toward the hall. Those voices were plain now—and angry. Then Silk's heart gave a jump because a sudden bellow of mixed rage and pain made the dishes in a china closet beside him rattle.

Only one man could roar like that— Butch!

Someone else said, "Hey Gus, I been watching the house next door every second. The lights are on, but I ain't seen nobody moving around. I ain't even noticed Mike casing the place. Maybe it is cops over there."

"Mike should have been back by now," the man called Gus snapped. "Three of you stay with this gorilla and the rest cover this whole house. Block the doors, search the rooms. Find out why we haven't heard from that half-wit we left at the back door to keep an eye on Mike. This smells like a trick to me; and we can't take chances now."

Silk glided into a small study, slipped around behind a door and waited, hardly daring to breathe. He'd walked straight into a hornet's nest all right. They'd find the door guard unconscious, Mike tied up in the yard and then—Silk shuddered—he'd join Butch in whatever kind of a devil's party he was undergoing.

To just stand there and wait for certain capture didn't appeal to Silk. He missed the Black Bat more than ever, but his one hope was to avenge the Black Bat's memory by taking a few of these thugs with him when he died.

Silk returned to the hallway cautiously, saw no one about, but heard the men searching upstairs and then a yell of surprise from the pair who had gone into the kitchen. Gus came rushing from the living room, tugging at his hip pocketed gun as he did so. The moment Gus vanished through the dining room door, Silk ran forward, turned into the living room and saw three startled thugs standings near a davenport on which Butch was firmly tied.

"Lift 'em!" Silk hissed. "Make it fast."

The three men raised their hands high. Silk moved forward a couple of more steps until he was within three feet of the trio. He made them turn around and then quickly disarmed them. He was fumbling in his pocket for a knife to cut Butch loose when a voice, high pitched with excitement, called a warning.

"Don't move, pal. I haven't got you covered, but there's a gun pushed right against your friend's skull. If you turn and try to shoot it out, he gets a slug first. Drop your gun and maybe we can talk things over."

SILK didn't move.

"You're lying," he retorted. "If it's a duel you want—you'll get it. I'm going to turn around and when I do—start shooting because that's what I'll be doing."

"You crackpot," the same voice rasped. "Look in the mirror across the room. See if I'm lying."

Silk raised his eyes and groaned. The leader of these thugs stood beside the davenport and his gun rested squarely in the middle of Butch's forehead. Silk lowered his automatic slowly. His fingers relaxed their grip and it fell to the rug.

Instantly the trio he'd held up, swung into action. One of them kicked the automatic away and the other two pounced on him. Silk was groggy and bleeding from several open cuts when they finally threw him into a chair. Butch, his eyes blazing wrath, said nothing, but Silk could see how the giant strained against the ropes that held him down.

Gus stepped up to Silk. "So you know this big lug, do you? That's great because we've been trying to make him talk ever since we got him, but the guy has a hide like an elephant's and half as many brains. Now —who is he and who are you? How'd you get wise to this hideout? Who do you work for?"

Silk had a nimble brain, but he couldn't think his way out of this mess. Playing for time wouldn't do him any good either because there was no help forthcoming anywhere. Carol couldn't do much. The police and G-Men were as ignorant of this hideout as they were of the Patriot's identity.

Mike came in, a lump on his forehead growing in size and color. He reached into his pocket and drew out a knife. The blade opened by touching a spring on the handle. It was a venomous looking piece of steel.

"I'll make him talk," Mike vowed. "I'll start slitting his throat inch by inch. Knock me out, will he?"

Other men entered. They reported that the house next door was empty and they'd extinguished the lights.

Gus said, "This bird turned on the lights to draw us out. We're safe! Mike—put that knife away. What difference does it make who these two guys are? Nobody else knows we're here or they'd be trying to crash the joint by now. So all we have to do is make sure these two never talk and —that's that."

Mike didn't put his knife away as ordered. He brought the razor-like edge within a hair's breadth of Silk's throat.

Gus snapped a command. "Either you stow the knife or I'll send a bullet through your thick head. I don't want any more marks on these two. The big guy is plenty bruised and the little one looks like he'd been put through a wringer too, but that won't matter because the sea does things like that to bodies that stay in the water a few hours."

"What's the gag?" Mike barked. "If they gotta be knocked off, let me do it. We'll weight them down . . . listen—a car!"

GUS cocked his head and turned slightly pale. Then a horn rapped out a peculiar signal and he relaxed.

"It's the boss. Douse all lights except that floor lamp. Turn the shade so the light is thrown into the faces of these two guys. The boss will want to see them. The rest of you guys beat it upstairs and don't come down until I call. Remember—anybody who lays eyes on the man who pays us off —gets his payoff in lead. Scram!"

Two minutes later only Gus remained in the room and he held a gun in his hand to keep Silk quiet. The front door lock clicked open, firm steps sounded across the floor and then there was a pause.

"What have you got here?" someone asked in a low, hollow voice that obviously was disguised for the benefit of the prisoners.

Gus explained. "The girl we captured and who got clear at the golf course house, went to see Kurt Miller. Miller phoned me because he knew she was a plant. We set a trap, figuring the girl would follow him if he went out, but instead we got this big guy. Next—the one in the chair sneaked in here—cleverly, too—but I nailed him. They won't talk so what's the use wasting time? I know a way that we can get rid of them."

"Good," the man in the darkness answered. "Tell me exactly how you propose to do it and hurry. I have a phone call to make. It is very important and these men must be out of here when I speak."

"It's easy. We've got bathing suits here—one that will even fit the gorilla. We strip both of them, put 'em in bathing trunks and keep 'em tied up, of course. The boys can take them down to the water, hold them under until they drown and then cut them loose. A row boat can take the bodies way out, dump 'em and they'll be washed ashore in a day or two. It'll look as though they fell out of a boat or swam beyond their limit and went under. Nothing to show it was murder."

"Excellent. I did well to select a man like you to guide the necessary brute strength we have had to employ. Do that—just as you described it to me. I am of the opinion that both these men worked for the Black Bat and are trying to carry out his plans. Later we shall see about the girl."

"Just step into the study and close the door," Gus said. "I'll get the boys down here and in fifteen minutes they'll have our prisoners in the water."

CHAPTER XIV

The Avenger in Black

GUS gave the orders and Silk was disrobed a n d bathing trunks put on him. Butch was cut loose by degrees and then retied b e f o r e he could do any damage. With four men assigned to e a c h doomed prisoner, they were carried out bodily.

As the door closed, Silk heard the

low, satisfied laughter of the Patriot. Silk was positive this newcomer was the brains behind the crime wave. He had tried to see beyond the halo of bright light thrown into his eyes for a look at the Patriot, but that had been impossible. The Patriot's voice meant nothing—even if he'd spoken in his natural tones—for Silk hadn't come into contact with any of the suspects and never heard them speak.

They were carried acoss the sand until water lapped at the feet of the eight murderers. Silk was dropped onto the wet sand and felt the surf wash lightly over him. He pulled with all his strength on those ropes. Even if they didn't break he hoped to leave marks that would remain after death and cause a medical examiner to have his suspicions about the manner of death.

One of the men said, "Mike—you get down there and bring back the dory. We'll do this fast."

Someone prodded Silk until he rolled over, closer and closer to the deep water. They kept this up until the sea filled Silk's mouth and nostrils. Butch was being similarly treated and his great body was performing violent twists and heaves to break the ropes.

"Okay," one man said. "Wade in with me and we'll hold them down for ten minutes. That ought to do the job right."

Rough hands seized Silk's legs and he was dragged beneath the water. In two or three minutes he'd be dead. Silk didn't mind that half as much as the fact that he'd utterly failed to avenge the Black Bat. He prayed that Carol would fade into obscurity before they got on her trail too. In all the Black Bat's history of fighting crime, he'd never come up against men as ruthless or clever as the Patriot. What could Carol do against a killer like him?

The dory, with a dark figure standing in the prow, drifted a little closer. A couple of the men looked up. Some-

one gave a startled scream. The others halted in their grisly tasks. Like rats they fled for dry land, clawing at their guns.

The figure in the dory had moved slightly and now the wind billowed out the black cape he wore until he looked like a huge bird. A bird that had flame spitting talons because the guns in his hands began dealing out justice.

With a leap, during which he seemed to actually fly, the man in black reached the beach and kept up his barrage. Three of the thugs were down. Another was crawling away, twisted in agony. The other four returned the fire, but their nerves were completely shattered.

The dead had arisen!

This was the Black Bat!

"We give up," someone shouted. "We give up. Don't shoot!"

"Drop your guns," came the order. "Get those two men out of the water. Quickly—if they're dead—all of you will die."

From the house came the roar of a car motor and tires scraped against the cinder drive. The Patriot and Gus were making good their escape, but that couldn't be helped. Silk and Butch were more important than that master of murder.

SILK sat up, blinked a few times and then almost lapsed into unconsciousness. The Black Bat moved toward him. The four remaining thugs were flat on their faces in the sand, arms outspread. The Black Bat cut Silk loose, pressed the knife into his hand and signaled he was to free Butch.

"Don't ask questions now," the Black Bat said in a satisfied voice. "I reached here in time. The Patriot got away—but that's all right, so long as you two are safe. What of Carol?"

"She's checking up on the King girl, sir." Silk was trying to bring Butch out of it. The big man had suffered more than Silk and probably been fighting so hard he forgot to fill his lungs with oxygen as the killers thrust him below water.

The Black Bat handed Silk a gun. "Watch those four—and the wounded one over there. The one called Mike, who went for the boat, is dead. He chose to fight and fell unconscious into the sea. I'll attend to Butch."

Butch opened his eyes a few moments later, looked straight up into the hooded face of the Black Bat and gave a long, satisfied grunt. Then he did a quick double take, sitting up and gaping at the man who rescued him.

"You're dead," he gulped. "You-you're dead. Then I must be dead too, huh? Only I don't get it. I'm still on the beach."

"And still alive—like me, Butch," the Black Bat said. "See if you can stand up. I need your help."

"Sure—sure, Boss." Butch got to his feet and almost collapsed. With a great effort, he gathered his strength and waited for orders.

"Those five men—one is wounded badly—are to be wrapped up for the police. While Silk holds a gun on them, use their clothing to tie them up. Do a good job, Butch."

"Oh, boy," Butch growled, "will I? Is that smart mug named Gus here too? He took a dozen swings at my nose while I was tied down and I'd like to hear how a rat's neck sounds when it busts."

"He's gone, Butch. These others are small fry, but the police won't mind meeting them. And Butch— don't try to make them talk because they have no more knowledge of the Patriot's real identity than you or I."

"Yeah—Gus made 'em all scram when the big shot showed up. Said if they saw him, they'd get rubbed out. Okay, boss, leave these lice to me. I'll fix 'em right."

The Black Bat made his way to the big house, found the door open and went in. He saw a telephone in the library, sat down behind the desk and then dialed for the operator. "Would you give me the charges on a call I just put through over this number, please?"

He was connected with long distance immediately and the Black Bat repeated his question.

"There was no overtime," the operator said. "A call to New York is twenty cents, sir."

"To New York?" the Black Bat asked with pretended amazement. "Are you sure we're both referring to the same call?"

"It was the last one made from that number, sir. You called Mandaley 6-9740."

"Thank you." The Black Bat hung up and sat back. He was still there when Butch and the first pair of crooks arrived, tucked beneath his big arms. He dropped them on the floor and grinned.

"Gosh, Boss, I thought I was dead. Honest I did. It was funny, too, because I didn't mind none when I saw you there too."

"That," the Black Bat said, "is a compliment. Now bring in the others. You'll find a car behind a big white oak a quarter of a mile down the road. Drive it here—and hurry—we have things to do."

WHEN all five of the men were laid out on the floor, the wounded member made as comfortable as possible, the Black Bat used the phone again and called New York police Headquarters. He asked for Captain McGrath and spoke in a natural tone.

"If you would like to see how a dead man rounds up certain members of the Patriot's band, why not pay a visit to James Halton's summer home at Pelham? I'm sure you'd be interested."

He heard McGrath give a half strangled cry. "Hey—don't hang up yet. You sound like the Black Bat, but you're not fooling me. The Black Bat is dead—lots of people saw him get blown completely to pieces."

The Black Bat chuckled softly. "Really, Captain, I'm all in one piece. Take my advice—come to Halton's summer home and bring an ambulance. One of the men has been injured. Oh yes—three others are dead. Not like me, Captain. They're really dead."

The Black Bat hung up, walked over to where the five men were lying on the floor and calmly pasted one of his stickers on the forehead of each one. Silk was doing the same thing outside—with the three dead crooks.

Not more than two minutes later the Black Bat, Silk and Butch were traveling back toward New York. Butch drove, but with his head twisted oddly so he could hear the Black Bat's story and still watch the road.

"It was close," the Black Bat admitted. "Much too close for comfort. When the fight started in the cottage on the cliff overlooking the river, I shot one man and he dropped. The others ran out and I started after them, but the crook I had a duel with had only been stunned by a ricocheting bullet.

"He came to and opened fire again. I batted him around a bit, knew that if I emerged with my outfit on, I'd be a perfect target so I changed clothes with the crook. My intentions were to get close enough to that lethal machine to wreck it—and some of the higher-ups who were nearby.

"Then it was you, dressed like one of those crooks, who came out and started running," Silk broke in. "The thug you'd knocked out recovered his senses, reached the doorway and began shooting at you. The blast came and—it was him I saw blown to bits."

"If you'd looked closer," the Black Bat removed his hood and grinned broadly, "you'd also have noticed me flying through the air with the greatest of ease. The blast tossed me to the cliff so I just kept on going and dived into the river.

"I knew I'd be declared dead and while I hated to let you, Butch and

Carol continue to think that, it was a perfect way to force the Patriot to get busy, and, perhaps, expose himself in doing so. I actually phoned the house twice, but nobody answered. I suppose all of you had left."

"But how did you happen to reach Halton's seashore home?" Silk asked. "You didn't trail the Patriot there, did you? You don't know who he is?"

"Unfortunately—no. His appearance was coincidental. I never expected him to show up. You see, after I dried myself I decided to follow a clue which had tantalized me for some time. Remember the man who was held prisoner at Kurt Miller's abandoned tenement house where the printing press was located? Of course you do.

WELL—he really had been held prisoner and I have identified him. He died in that blast at the airport, but he wasn't trying to sabotage those planes. I'm certain of that. All he wanted to do was warn them of impending danger. In the cab that he rode, I discovered ink smears. I found more of them in the old tenement house. Obviously the man's hands had been covered with ink—which tied up with the printing machine.

"I looked for a printer who probably had a small place of his own, and was missing for a couple of days.

"The police helped me via the telephone, though they had no idea of it. The dead man was named Herbert Marks. He received a call one night a few days ago, that he was wanted for a special job. The caller asked if he was alone and Marks, somewhat suspicious, said yes. In reality his wife also was present. He was told to report at once to Halton's summer home. The caller offered a sizeable sum for his trouble and indicated the work was to be done secretly."

"And Marks fell for it," Silk sighed. "He went to Halton's summer home and they made him print those phony newspaper outer pages on a press they'd installed in Miller's vacant tenement. Marks deserves a lot of credit for what he tried to do."

"Naturally I paid a visit to Halton's place and found you and Butch. All of which leaves us almost exactly where we were before," the Black Bat said. "True, we've broken up the Patriot's mob rather well, but he can easily get more men. I have a couple of clues, one of which is just a phone number and might fizzle out.

"I was able to do a little investigating, though, especially in connection with the two explosions, one at the airport and the other on the river.

"I discovered that after Marks was blown to bits, the authorities naturally became suspicious and examined the three doomed planes very thoroughly. Then, after that was done, the cameras were loaded aboard. The torpedo boats, likewise were gone over and then—speedometers were t a k e n aboard. I think something connected with those cameras and speedometers is responsible for the blasts.

Right now though, we'd better head for home as fast as possible— without getting pinched, Butch—so that when Captain McGrath comes around to prove that Tony Quinn is dead, he'll find a live corpse."

"Perhaps," Silk added gently, "Carol might also be responsible for the speed you want, sir?"

"Exactly, Silk. Exactly."

CHAPTER XV

The Patriot's Move

MEANWHILE, Carol forced all thoughts of Tony Quinn out of her mind. She'd been well trained by the Black Bat and knew exactly how to approach a house without being seen herself. Luckily, she carried out her training well for as she neared Viola King's cottage, she saw dark forms in a field two or three hundred yards from the house.

Carol circled them, getting closer to Joel King's workshop at the rear. Her intentions were to search for clues—anything that might prove or disprove that Halton possessed the greatest possibility of being the Patriot. Like the others, she was more or less convinced of his guilt.

Crawling through the high grass, she encountered a wire, avoided it completely and then suddenly realized just what it meant. G-Men or Police had tapped Viola King's phone —perhaps also installed a dictaphone. They had run the wire into the field and were listening there now.

An encounter with them would be embarrassing. She reached the workshop, made certain no police were inside and stepped in herself. With a small flash, shaded by her hands, she inspected the premises. Five minutes passed to no avail. Then a telephone, hooked to the wall beside the door, suddenly jangled and made Carol break out in a cold sweat. She hurried to the phone, carefully lifted the receiver and as she placed the instrument to her ear, someone in the house also answered.

"Viola?" a man's voice inquired.

"Father!" Viola King gasped. "Father—are you all right?"

"Perfectly all right, my child," the man replied. "Don't worry about me. We're going to be rich, Viola. More money than we ever dreamed about."

"The—invention?" Viola a s k e d breathlessly. "Dad—you can't sell it. You didn't make it for that purpose. You never even told me you'd perfected it. Dad—what's come over you?"

"An influence," the man answered blithely. "It's called money. A very clever man pointed out to me how we can all make a lot of money. No more of that struggling for an existence. And—better yet—it can be done without the slightest bit of suspicion being thrown on me. I'll return and say I was kidnaped."

"But you were, Dad—you must have been. Think of what you're doing. Think of me."

"I have been, my dear. I was kidnaped and I had my choice of co-operating or being killed. When I demonstrated my invention, the Patriot—as he calls himself—promised to let me share in the profits. Did you see those planes go down, those torpedo boats smashed to bits, and that fool at the airport who was blown to kingdom come?

"That was my invention at work, Viola. Those men had to die so I might prove the capabilities of the device. I'm satisfied—so is the Patriot—and the government soon will be. Unless they are utter fools and refuse to deal with us. In that case we have someone else bidding for it."

VIOLA half screamed. "You can't do that. You can't! You're an American. Please, Dad—give the invention to the government. Please —they'll never let us rest if you don't."

"Bosh," came the chiding reply. "In this world it's every man for himself. I'm convinced of the Patriot's policies. Now listen carefully: I was permitted to phone you for two reasons. First, to assure you I'm safe and well. Secondly, to warn you that very soon now we'll require your aid. The instructions you will receive must be carried out. Do you understand, Viola? If you fail—I'll be killed."

"I-I'll do as you say." Viola was crying bitterly. "Perhaps we can work something out when you're free. Be careful, Dad. I . . ."

The connection was cut off. Carol leaned limply against the wall. The Patriot was getting ready to strike. Joel King worked with him; and now his daughter was forced into the plot. G-Men, probably, had overheard the conversation and would be ready to move in on them promptly.

Carol felt utterly lost. Unless Silk and Butch had dug up something, the case had reached an impasse. The Patriot had covered up his tracks and there was nothing left to do but wait. When his demands came, perhaps they'd find some way to circumvent the man.

Carol peered through a window, saw the men in the field moving toward the street. She went out and hurried away into the night. There was nothing for her to do at Viola King's. The girl was probably just as miserable as Carol right now.

She drove to Tony Quinn's house, left the car up the street and reached the lab through its tunnel. Butch was there. The big man sprang to his feet as Carol entered. He grasped both her shoulders and looked down into her eyes.

"Easy now," he said and his face was wreathed in the biggest grin Carol had ever seen. "I got somethin' to tell you. Swell news, Carol. He's okay!"

"He's—okay?" Carol repeated the two words very slowly. Then she grasped Butch's big arms. "Butch— what are you trying to tell me? You mean Tony—he isn't . . . ?"

"Sh-h-h," Butch cautioned. "He's in there right now—with Captain Mc-Grath. I'll open the secret door just a crack. Silk parked McGrath with his back to the door on purpose. Take a look!"

Carol's hand shot to her mouth to stop the glad cry that rose involuntarily to her lips. Tony Quinn, clad in his smoking jacket, with his pipe between his teeth, sightless eyes staring at the fireplace, was listening to McGrath.

The Detective Captain hadn't quite recovered from the shock of finding Tony Quinn at home—alive.

"Okay, okay," McGrath said for the third time. "I admit that if the Black Bat really is dead, I was all wrong about you. But listen to this—somebody phoned me about an hour ago. Said he was the Black Bat and, so help me, he sounded like him. I was told to make tracks for Jim Halton's summer home in Pelham and, believe me, I travelled.

"When I got there, I found four of the Patriot's mugs tied up and another wounded. On the beach were three more—dead. They were all branded—with the Black Bat's stickers. Now I saw him blown to bits with my own eyes. Maybe you got an idea about that, Mr. Quinn?"

QUINN asked casually: "I'm afraid not. If you saw the Black Bat killed—then he must either have a double, or an imposter is at work."

"Yeah—only the five crooks who were still alive swore the Black Bat just came sailing toward them in a boat. They claim he flew at them, too —like a bird. Those guys were so scared they talked their heads off and we learned—just nothing. They worked for the Patriot and they say he has got a machine that can blast things off the map; but that's all they knew. Not one of 'em ever saw the Patriot."

"And why would they know him?" Quinn argued. "A man as clever as the Patriot wouldn't entrust such knowledge to strong-armed, weak-minded thugs as they. And Captain —when you came in here and saw me, you actually believed then that the Black Bat wasn't dead.

"You're convinced I'm the Black Bat and you shook hands with me so often and so hard my fingers still are numb. Really, despite all the threats you make, I think you'd be delighted if you were certain the Black Bat was alive. Confess now —wouldn't you?"

McGrath looked at the tip of his cold cigar and grinned feebly.

"Well now that you put it that way—I dunno—I felt like a heel after I thought he was dead. Sure he's a law breaker and he ought to be flung into a cell, but he has done a lot of good too. Anyway he is dead. I'm —I think he's dead. I opened up, Quinn. You come through now and admit you're the Black Bat. On my honor, I won't do a thing about it."

Quinn laughed. "But Captain— how many times have you tested me? You've even brought doctors here to examine my eyes. I'm blind! Could the Black Bat operate as he does, bereft of his sight? No, Captain, you're on the wrong track as usual. I'm afraid . . ."

The phone rang and Silk hurried to answer it. He carried the instrument over to where McGrath sat, plugged it into a convenient socket.

"For you, Captain."

McGrath barked a greeting and then did a lot of listening. When he hung up, his face was flushed.

"Look here," he said to Quinn, "you're Viola King's lawyer. Maybe you're the Black Bat too, but right now I'm speaking to you as an attorney. That call was from a G-Man. They tapped the phone wires to Viola King's house. There's some kind of a law against doing that, but in this case all rules are suspended. They picked up a conversation between Viola and her father.

"So he isn't dead—he's alive and helping the Patriot. He may even be the Patriot himself. Viola has been named as the go-between and she is to receive orders later."

Quinn slowly removed the pipe from his lips. "So that's the method the Patriot intends to employ. It places Viola in a dangerous situation. Yet, what can she or anyone else do about it?"

McGrath arose. "The Patriot sure seems to hold all the cards. Well— I've got to get busy. All I hope is that the Black Bat isn't dead. I've never hoped for anything so much in my life."

After McGrath had gone, Quinn entered the lab. Carol rushed into his arms, her eyes, tear stained, yet shining in the light of complete happiness.

Finally Quinn said, "The case rapidly is building up to a point where the Patriot is gong to get his money or find himself in a cell on Death Row."

"Tony," Carol said, "I overheard a phone call between Viola and her father. . . . "

QUINN sat down beside her. "McGrath just learned all about it too. That call was made from Halton's summer home during the time when I was busy saving Butch and Silk. Joel King must have been concealed in the house somewhere, never permitted to come into contact with any visitors, welcome or unwelcome. And, incidentally, there goes my clue —the telephone number which was called at Halton's place.

"I hoped it might lead me to something more definite than Viola King. Just before McGrath arrived Silk checked the number so I wasn't particularly surprised when McGrath told me that story—which you have further verified, Carol."

"But what are we going to do?" Carol asked. "If Viola King helps her father and through him, the Patriot, she'll be in terrible danger. No matter which way it turns out, the police or those crooks will be after her."

Quinn nodded. "I know, but if she has been appointed as the go-between, we can't stop it. I'll see her as soon as I can—find out what her orders are and it's possible we'll find something to work on there. It's our only chance. . . . "

Silk opened the secret door and interrupted him. "A car just pulled up, sir. You'd better come out."

Quinn picked up his cane, smiled at Carol and hurried into the next room. He sat down, his eyes filmed over and he started puffing on his pipe again.

Silk let two people in—Viola King and Hank Standish. Both were considerably agitated. Silk announced them, helped Viola into a chair near Quinn and then discreetly withdrew.

Quinn said, "I'm very glad you came, Viola. I wanted you to see me of your own accord. I know all about your being appointed as the Patriot's agent. I know your father isn't dead, but appears to be working with the Patriot. I learned all this from the police."

"What shall I do?" Viola begged. "It's my father. They'll kill him if I don't obey and if I do—it means the Patriot will have won."

Quinn gave her some advice. "It is your father, Viola. In some countries all allegiance must be made to the state. Family ties are thrown away, but this is the United States where, fortunately, we respect our parents and try to help them. If you refuse to obey the Patriot's orders, your father will be murdered. Your gesture will be vain anyhow because it would be a simple matter for that crook to get someone else. He has chosen you because he can trust you, and he has a hold over you."

"No," Hank Standish suddenly shouted. "I disagree. This matter concerns the entire world. It isn't just Joel King. He is working with those crooks and doesn't deserve any sympathy. I say Viola should keep out of it—that she should tell the police everything, work in unison with them if necessary."

VIOLA sighed deeply. "Hank and I have been arguing about it for an hour, Mr. Quinn. I felt as you did and now I'm convinced. I shall obey the Patriot, do precisely what he asks."

"Then you don't have to wonder why I'm not dropping in to see you any more," Hank Standish roared. "They'll kill your father no matter what you do to help them. People like the Patriot don't split their take with anyone else. You're being a fool and this attorney is—well his eyes aren't the only sightless thing about him. His brain is just as blind."

Hank Standish grabbed his hat and strode to the door. Silk let him out and disappeared again.

Viola was crying softly. Quinn asked her questions calculated to stop those tears.

"Tell me — do you really believe your father perfected this death machine? Was there any evidence that he had finished it?"

Viola dabbed at her eyes again. "I—don't know. Dad kept me in school all the time. He even refused to allow me to come home during vacations—said he was too busy to see me. I came home unannounced one day and I found him in the laboratory. I wanted to surprise him so I looked in the window first. He had a rabbit—in a cage. There was a funny looking thing pointed at the rabbit. Then, when I entered the laboratory—the cage was empty and there were no signs of the rabbit. Father never mentioned anything about this to me."

"And you came home this time also unannounced?"

"Yes—I begged him to let me come back, but he didn't even answer my letter. So I came along without his permission. Except for that day or two a year ago, it was the first time I'd been home in four years. I didn't know anyone — the neighbors had changed—everything was different. It wasn't like home any more."

"Tell me," Quinn asked, "the night those men appeared—just what happened? Standish told me he recognized none of them."

"Those men came. Hank tried to—to prevent them from coming in and they tied him up. They shoved me into a clothes closet. I heard Mr. Halton cry out and that was all until —the Black Bat came."

"And Standish told you the same story, Viola? I must know the truth. It is very important."

Viola looked at the floor for a moment. "He did recognize someone.

It was—my father. Hank swore it was. He said Dad went to the safe, opened it and took out some papers. He told me he didn't admit this to anyone because he—wanted to protect me."

Quinn arose and she stepped to his side. He said, "Go home now and stay there until you hear from the Patriot. If you wish to ask my advice—or even tell me what he has ordered, feel free to do so. In fact it might be best if you did tell me."

"I—mean to tell the police," Viola said. "Unless you advise against it."

"I do—very much. Your father's life depends on this and we must save him somehow. By freeing him you will not only benefit yourself, but also the government. Your father knows the secret of that machine. He could build another. Good night, Viola."

CHAPTER XVI

Headquarters Conference

NEXT day, during the first matinee performances in several movie theatres in the Times Square district, patrons received more than their money's worth. When the news films began, they were suddenly interrupted by a glaring title indicating that the next scene would show the three torpedo boats being destroyed. The pictures of their finish were clear and painfully vivid. Then, while the scene repeated itself again and again, a man's voice spoke.

"You have just witnessed what the greatest weapon in the world can do. Nothing is safe from it. I am the Patriot. I have demanded twenty million dollars from your government for the secret of this device. That offer still goes, but there is not much time left. While statesmen dicker and argue, another great power has offered me twenty-five millions of dollars in cash.

"However, I did not name myself the Patriot because I liked the sound of that word. I really have the welfare of our nation in my heart—provided they pay for the article I possess. Therefore, through you and everyone else who witnesses these pictures and hears my voice, I say to the authorities a token payment of a million dollars in small bills—fives, tens and twenties — must be neatly done up in small bundles and delivered to—Miss Viola King—before nine o'clock tonight!

"I shall consider it a token payment made in good faith. She will receive her own instructions and if she is interfered with, or this offer refused, I shall once more indicate how powerful my weapon is. The Acme Insurance Company Building will be blasted to its base. That is my warning. See that those men you have elected to represent you, heed it."

There was a meeting at noon in Commissioner Warner's office. Government officials, G-Men, Halton and Lockwood were present. So was Tony Quinn, whom Silk led in and helped to a chair.

Warner said, "Finally the Patriot has issued definite instructions. A token payment of a million dollars must be delivered to Viola King before tonight at nine. Mr. Halton, you flew from Washington where you had a conference with executives this morning. What do you suggest?"

"That we pay it—every penny. That we deliver the money to Viola King and withdraw, allow her to proceed with whatever instructions she receives. To try to trap the Patriot might result in a catastrophe."

Lockwood stepped forward. "On the surface of it, Halton seems right. He has argued the point in Washington and he has told me the money is available. A million dollars isn't too much to risk and it will stall the Patriot from exhibiting the powers of his infernal machine, or his turning it over, to another country. I think we should follow Halton's advice."

THE Director of the local Field Office of the F.B.I. banged his fist on the desk top.

"I don't. Every time we let the Patriot get away with something, he'll become that much more sure of himself and make further demands. For this token payment of a million dollars he promises us nothing. My opinion is that the money should be turned over to Miss King, but she is to be kept under observation and when she makes contact with the Patriot or his men, we can move in."

Warner looked over at Quinn. "What do you think about it, Tony?"

Quinn shrugged. "I'm Viola King's attorney and I must look on the matter from her point of view. Her father's life is threatened. Her own too, probably, if she fails to carry out these orders. As her attorney I agree with Halton. As a citizen of the United States, speaking off the record as a lawyer, I say go after the Patriot with everything you've got. If I were District Attorney, I would certainly not hesitate to take advantage of any situation through which I could get at the Patriot."

"Don't listen to him," Halton yelled shrilly. "What does he know about matters like this? Anyway, gentlemen, it is quite out of your hands. The payment will be made. Miss King is not to be followed nor interfered with. We need a breathing spell during which you so-called protectors of the law can find a clue. We can get it by paying off."

"Just a moment," Warner flushed angrily, "before you criticize the police and other law agencies, perhaps you will explain why the Patriot's men used your summer home as a hideout."

"What?" Halton gaped. "My summer home? Good heavens, I didn't know that. I swear it. Lockwood—

why didn't you tell me? After all, the place practically is yours."

Lockwood took a long puff on his cigarette. "I didn't know about it, Halton. It's true that I have made arrangements to take title to the place, that I have keys to it and you no longer recognize the property as your own, but this is as much of a surprise to me as it is to you."

"What difference does it make?" Halton bellowed. "The Patriot might have used anyone's home as his headquarters. The fact remains that he possesses an instrument which can create havoc with the world. He demands an exorbitant price, but we're spending billions on armaments that will be made absolutely useless against his device.

"We must gain possession of this machine. How will you gentlemen feel if he turns it on the Acme Insurance Company Building, as he has threatened? Hundreds of people will be killed—their blood on your heads. And that will be just the beginning. The Patriot is going to be paid off."

Halton jerked his head toward the door for Lockwood's benefit and they both stalked out. Warner sat down and shook his head from side to side.

"He's right, of course. Our hands are tied. We've encountered the greatest criminal on record and—met our match. Anyway, t h i s meeting must not be made public. I don't know what the police will do—yet."

The G-Man Field Director arose. "I know what my men and I will do. We'll watch Viola King, trail her and try to intercept the delivery of that money. This too, is a secret, gentlemen. If it leaks out, we shall know someone in this office is responsible. Let me know your decision, Commissioner, so we can work together if you wish it that way."

WHEN only Quinn and Silk were left in the office, Warner relaxed a bit.

"Tony," he said, "I wonder what

the Black Bat would do under these circumstances? He's supposed to be dead—I'd take my oath on that—but Captain McGrath claims he isn't. I hope McGrath is right because if anyone can save this situation, the Black Bat can."

Quinn signaled Silk who helped him up and piloted him in front of Warner's desk.

"I don't know about that, Commissioner," Quinn said, "but I do believe some attempt should be made to trace the money Viola King will deliver.

That's up to you. I'm utterly helpless. Let me know what happens, will you? I still have a client to protect and don't forget—you brought her to me."

Going down the steps of Police Headquarters, Quinn spoke to Silk.

"Is my good friend, Steve Cobb, still hanging around with his cab? Interesting fellow, Steve. Swears he'll chauffeur me from now on."

"I don't know what you see in that guy," Silk growled. "He looks just like a dumb hack driver to me and that crate of his isn't exactly the lap of luxury to ride in either."

"Just the same I'm letting him drive us home," Quinn said. "After all, he can't pay me in cash so let him think he's paying off by catering to my wants."

Steve Cobb brushed Silk aside and aided Quinn into his cab. "Thanks, Steve," Quinn said, "and say—stick around today, will you? Things are going to pop and I might find it necessary to go places fast. Leave your meter on—I'll pay the charges."

"I'll be there whenever you want," Steve Cobb vowed, "and the meter ain't goin' to be tickin' either. Where to now, boss? Home?"

CHAPTER XVII

The Patriot's Trick

VIOLA KING received an unaddressed letter slipped beneath her door shortly before three o'clock. At seven that night Jim Halton and Lockwood appeared. They were accompanied by four heavily armed men who took up advantageous stations to cover the house. Halton and Lockwood carried four compact bundles with them. A million dollars, in small bills, unmarked and without numbers noted. Halton had insisted on this.

Viola King seemed almost lost in the big chair she occupied. Halton arranged the packages carefully on a table.

"Remember—the amount of money inside those wrappers is tremendous. We're entrusting it to your care because we must. You have heard from the Patriot?"

"Yes—a letter. I—I don't think I should tell you what it said. Mr. Quinn advised me. . . ."

"Mr. Quinn be hanged," Halton barked. "This is a government matter — nothing for a blind man to handle. Don't tell anyone what is in that letter—not even me. Carry out your instructions and if anything happens, let me know instantly. We'll be going now—so that there will be no interference with what you have to do. Good night, Miss King."

Viola King sat staring at the bundles of money after Halton and Lockwood had gone. She glanced at a clock on the mantlepiece, saw that she had plenty of time and stayed in that chair until seven-thirty. Then she hastily donned her hat and a coat. Carrying the four bundles of money to the back door, she left them there temporarily while she got the car out of the garage and drove it up beside the back porch. Then she made two trips with the money, placing it into the rear seat.

When she rolled out of the driveway, a G-Man spoke sharply into a neighbor's telephone anent her departure. At the next corner a car pulled out and followed at a discreet distance. It was equipped with a two-way radio and contained five men—three F.B.I. agents, Captain McGrath and another ranking police officer.

"Keep well back," McGrath warned. "Maybe some of the Patriot's men will start trailing her. If they do—we grab them, and fast. Hey—she's heading for the outskirts."

They rode in silence then, every man intent on watching the cheap car which Viola drove. She crossed the city line, keeping to the busy highway. Captain McGrath frequently spoke into the two-way radio system and every available police and G-Man car was tuned in. A mighty cordon was in the preparation of being thrown around whatever area Viola stopped in.

Suddenly the girl pulled over, about a hundred yards away from one of the busiest highway intersections in the state. Three distinct roads met here and the center of the intersection was controlled by an elaborate system of rotary traffic.

McGrath spoke into the radio again. "All cars—converge on Three Point Corner. Subject has stopped there. Cover each road, every lane. Stand by for complete description of contacting car."

The five men drew guns. McGrath even removed a submachine rifle from its sleeve on the roof of the car. Still nothing happened. Viola apparently just sat waiting.

They saw a hearse roll past them, saw its brake lights wink, but no one paid much attention to it until the hearse pulled up directly beside Viola's car.

The rear door swung open and two men got out. Both had coat collars pulled high and hat brims down over their eyes. They entered Viola's car, came out in less than ten seconds and held something close against their bodies. They made one more trip and then jumped into the back of the hearse. It pulled away and McGrath gave the signal to attack.

The police car roared forward. One man jumped out as it slowed a bit, and went to Viola's car to protect her. The others tore after the hearse. The grim black vehicle turned left. So did the driver of McGrath's car. Guns were raised now, ready to let fly a song of death. Then McGrath's jaw dropped, someone rasped a curse and they all saw their chances of capturing that hearse flitting away like a puff of steam.

In his first swift count, McGrath checked eleven hearses all practically alike and matching the one which had been manned by the Patriot's men. Each lane of traffic disgorged more of them.

Sirens were wailing from all directions now as police cars closed in to block the highways.

It required a full hour to assemble all the hearses. Their drivers and attendants were none too polite about how they felt either.

"We got a hurry call," one driver explained. "The address was phony so we just turned around and started for home."

Another indicated that he was on his way to pick up a corpse. Each hearse was owned by a reputable undertaker, the drivers and attendants were checked and found to be telling the truth. There were twenty-three hearses in all now and their number increasing every two or three minutes as police herded others to the spot.

Not one carried a single clue to the whereabouts of the missing cash. The Patriot again had won. He'd even foreseen that the police and G-Men would try to move in on him.

McGrath walked back to his car.

"How many people knew we were going to trail the King girl? Halton, Lockwood, Quinn and his valet, Silk. The last two are okay—take my word on that. But Halton has been yelling his head off about paying the Patriot. He maneuvered this whole thing. Lockwood has always been with him, maybe egging him on. It's Lockwood or Halton. Personally I think it's Lockwood because he's kept his mouth shut and he's a smart bird."

"Let's pick both of them up," the Field Director of the F.B.I. suggested. "You see to that, Captain. I'll take charge of protecting the Acme Insurance Building. Don't forget—the Patriot promised to blow it to bits if we crossed him and we certainly showed our hand plainly here. I think the hearse actually manned by the Patriot's men made good its escape right through our cordon. Anyway the Acme Building is our greatest worry right now."

TONY QUINN heard about the events from two sources. Commissioner Warner called and described what had happened and almost the moment Quinn hung up, Viola King was on the wire.

"The police were there—G-Men too," she sobbed. "What will happen now—to Dad, I mean? They'll think I warned the police. They'll kill him."

"Please," Quinn soothed her, "nothing like that will happen. If you had told the police, they'd have captured those men easily. The Patriot knows that. Just sit tight—don't talk to anyone. If you receive further advice from the Patriot, let me know about it. And don't worry — your father is going to be all right."

When Quinn hung up, S i l k grunted: "Trust McGrath to pull a stunt like that. He flops every time he tries anything. Of course the Patriot will murder Viola's father now.

What's more, he'll blow up one of the big buildings in town. People will be killed."

"A building will not be blown up, people will not be killed and the Patriot is on his way to justice," Quinn said softly. "Don't ask questions because I'm not prepared to answer them. However—in a short time we're all going into action.

"For days I've kept a card up my sleeve, not daring to use it because if I failed—well, I'd be sunk, too. Now it's time to play that card, but first we'll wait. The Patriot won't take this fiasco lying down. We'll hear from him, in one way or another. Meanwhile you'd better get your disguise materials ready for quick application."

That Tony Quinn spoke the truth became evident an hour later. Captain McGrath arrived, face flushed, eyes hard and uncompromising. He had a piece of paper in his hand.

"Warner sent me over with· this," McGrath barked. "Take a look at it."

Quinn never even moved his head, nor allowed a muscle in his arms to ripple.

"I?" he smiled wanly. "Come now, Captain, you know better than that. Forever trying to trick me into betraying the fact that I can't see, aren't you? Hand it to Silk and he'll read the thing to me. What is it, anyway?"

"I'm sorry." McGrath sat down like a man dead on his feet. "I wasn't trying to trick you. So many things have happened, there's so much to do —I just forgot. This is a leaflet, one of several thousand that came floating down from several different tall buildings in town. It's the Patriot's latest blast. Read it, Silk."

Silk did. "The heading says, 'PATRIOT DEFIANT.' Then it goes on, sir. 'Despite all my warnings the Police and G-Men disobeyed the orders I gave and tried to intercept certain cash being paid to me by government officials smart enough to realize I hold the upper hand.

" 'Because of this fact I now demand the instant payment of another sum —three million dollars to be delivered to me by tomorrow night and if any attempts are made to intercept the men sent for it—the weapon I now own will be immediately sold to certain agents of another government. It will be turned against us eventually because the nation that possesses it can rule the world.

" 'I made a promise that I would exhibit my little machine again if I was crossed. Now I am forced to do that. I hereby warn everyone to remain away from the vicinity of the Acme Insurance Company Building. If my new demands are not met I shall take steps to destroy a battleship now in the harbor.

" 'Citizens—contact your duly elected representatives. Tell them they must obey me. It is foolish to attempt any compromise or to defy me.' "

"Patriot!" McGrath growled derisively. "He's the biggest traitor we've ever known. For the love of Mike, Mr. Quinn, if you have any ideas about this—if you are the Black Bat—help us."

QUINN disregarded McGrath's plea. "What have you done about the Acme Building?"

"Everything possible. Cleared it out, searched every nook and cranny —at least that's being done now. And say, listen to this, Jim Halton and George Lockwood both have offices in that building. Coincidence, maybe? Not to me it isn't. One of those two —or maybe both—are connected with the Patriot. Anyway we're doing all we can. Buildings nearby are watched. Nobody is allowed to enter. The streets are patroled and guarded. But what good is all this if a machine can be set up somewhere, maybe quite far away, and turn some kind of a blast on the building? We can't cover the whole city."

"True," Quinn agreed. "But it's

still your problem, Captain. Thanks for bringing me the latest dope sheet from the Patriot. One thing about that man—he likes himself."

When Silk returned from letting McGrath out, Tony Quinn had disappeared into the private laboratory. He rarely moved in such haste immediately after McGrath departed so Silk knew things were ripe for action.

Carol and Butch were there. Quinn opened a large cabinet and gestured toward the small arsenal it contained.

"Arm yourselves—bring extra ammunition. Carol, we'll use your car because it's big and fast. You and Butch drive to the corner, pick up Silk and follow me. I'll be in Steve Cobb's taxi. Stay out of sight until I signal."

Quinn left the lab and Butch and Carol looked at Silk inquisitively. Silk shrugged and kept dabbing on makeup.

"He says he's going to play an ace that's been up his sleeve for a few days. Don't ask me what it is. I'd better go help him."

Quinn put on his coat, picked up his cane and hat and moved to the door. At the curb, Steve Cobb was dozing behind the wheel of his taxi. He woke up instantly when Quinn walked down the steps. Cobb rushed up to him and helped him to the taxi.

"Gosh, boss," Steve Cobb said, "somethin' must have happened. I can tell by your face. Where to?"

"Viola King's house—where you took me before. Hurry, Steve, this is urgent. The Patriot is getting ready to spring his last trap. The Police practically are wise to him and they've set a little trap of their own."

"Yeah?" Steve gaped. "Say—can I get in on the excitement?"

"Nobody can," Quinn replied. "Captain McGrath just left my house. Anyway they've rigged up something at the Acme Insurance Company Building that is bound to nail anyone who enters. Just what it is I must keep secret, but—it will work. If it does —the Patriot or his agents will be

killed. Every one of them. I've got to warn Viola not to stir. She's a peculiar girl and might decide to visit the building and challenge the Patriot."

"Okay," Steve gasped and drove like a mad man to Viola King's home. He even mounted the curb before he got the car to a stop. Quinn was all but dragged out.

"You gonna be in there a few minutes, boss?" Steve asked breathlessly. "I gotta make a phone call down the street. Won't take me long."

"Very well," Quinn answered, "but I won't be here more than three or four minutes and I'll need you badly. You only know half of what's going to happen tonight, Steve."

THE taxi shot away and Carol's car glided up softly. Tony Quinn cast aside all pretense of being blind. He jumped into the car, peeled off his hat and coat and hurriedly donned the somber clothing of the Black Bat.

"Follow Steve," he told Carol. "Don't lose him whatever you do. He won't be suspicious. The little man is in far too much of a hurry to think about anything other than a very mythical trap which the police are setting for the Patriot."

"I don't understand, sir," Silk frowned.

Quinn laughed. "Steve Cobb was my ace in the hole. That's why I permitted, even encouraged, him to hang around. You see Steve happens to be an agent of the Patriot, assigned to watch me. Just why, I'm not so sure except that it's possible they think I'm working very closely with the police and transferring to them a lot of information I get from Viola. At any rate, Steve is not only the Patriot's agent—he's a murderer."

"Murderer?" Carol cried. "Whom did he kill?"

"The printer who was blown to bits at the airfield. I've been sure of that ever since I learned the facts. Think back—the printer got away very neatly. In fact, I think they let him get away. He knew what they were up to because he printed those circulars under their direction. Probably they even told him that if he escaped he could save the lives of those pilots by going directly to the airport."

"But where does Steve come in?" Silk asked.

"The printer jumped through a window, fell and was hurt. We know that. Steve and his taxi came along at the crucial moment and of course the printer pressed Steve into service. He drove the printer to the airport and from the testimony of sentries at the gate and from Steve himself, even helped the printer out and up to the gate. The man was injured and needed this help. But Steve was sending him to his doom."

"How?" Butch and Silk chorused.

"You'll learn that quickly enough. Now—watch him. No time to talk. Steve will go directly to the Patriot's headquarters. He's bound to because of what I told him. Then we must act fast."

CHAPTER XVIII

Raid

STEVE really did that trip up brown, flirting with arrest at every traffic light. Carol kept on his trail, far enough behind to avoid being seen, but always maintaining a constant distance between the two cars.

Quinn now was garbed in his regalia and had become the Black Bat once more. Steve led them across town and then up Riverside Drive. Suddenly his tail light flashed as the car made a quick turn into a driveway. Carol immediately slowed up.

"He entered that estate," the Black Bat said. "Carol—drive close to it, and I'll get out. You others park the car, return and be ready to fight your way inside. Don't make any more noise than necessary until the fireworks really begin. Good luck!"

He leaped out of the car as it slowed down, flitted across the sidewalk so fast that he was a darker blur among many shadows. Few people were on the streets and he went unnoticed.

About fifty yards up the imposing driveway was an iron gate. The Black Bat ducked off the drive, merged with the carefully cultivated shrubbery and approached the gate carefully.

He held a gun in his hand and those extremely sensitive ears of his were alert for the slightest sound. He heard a hoarse whisper, parted branches and his eyes cleaved the darkness to see two men standing beside the gate. Both had submachine guns.

He veered left, reached the fence at a point well away from the gate and took a slender piece of steel from his pocket. Ordinarily it was used to pry open locks, but this time the black Bat tossed it lightly at the fence. There was no crackle of electricity and he felt secure in climbing the fence. That was no easy task for it had been made to circumvent any such attempts.

He crouched, for a moment, on top of the fence and then jumped. Ordinary eyes would not have seen the small, cleared area below, but the Black Bat saw it and avoided being tangled up in shrubs.

He had to work fast. Silk, Butch and Carol would be on their way toward the gate in a few moments. Running lightly, he reached the drive. Rubber soled shoes on well cropped lawn were noiseless and the two guards had no inkling that an enemy approached until one of them suddenly groaned and slumped to the ground.

The other started to turn around. He saw a blur that turned into a fist. It walloped him on the chin, stifled the cry for help and stunned his brain. Another punch finished him off.

The Black Bat searched both men, removed their guns and found keys to the gate in the pockets of one. He unlocked the big iron doors and in a moment his three aides were gathered about him.

"The Patriot's real headquarters are in the mansion. You can see the rooftop above the trees. Our job is to get inside and save Joel King. The Patriot may have quite a group of killers assembled here so make every shot count if shooting becomes necessary.

"Carol—you are to remain here. Don't argue the point—someone must. Watch for any signs of reinforcements. Give us about ten minutes and then come immediately to the rear door of the house. Keep out of sight until you see one of us. Watch these two guards also and use the butt of your gun on them if they start making any noise."

WITH Silk and Butch close beside him, to take advantage of his abnormal sight, the Black Bat moved quickly toward the house. They surveyed the place, huge and sprawling, one of the last remnants of an era gone by.

"We can't delay a moment," the Black Bat warned. "Getting into the place won't be easy, but I'm afraid they may murder Joel King if they have time to do so. Therefore, this is our plan. Butch, reach the west side of the house. Silk you take the east and I'll tackle the rear.

"Check your watches with mine— just let me see them—I'll adjust them for you in the darkness. Now, in precisely four minutes I want each of you to hurl the biggest rock you can find through a window. I'll do the same. The killers inside won't be sure from what direction the crash came.

"I'm hoping that they all rush to either side of the house so I can go in through the back. When I get there—and my chances are two-to-one against my making it—I'll start another diversion which will draw them to my side. You two will then try to get in also."

"I understand sir." Silk's face was set.

Butch smiled grimly. "Me too, this is what I been waitin' for. It's okay to slug as many of them rats as I can, huh?"

"It's just what I want you to do," the Black Bat said. "All right, we part up here. Four minutes—on the dot."

The Black Bat made his way to the rear of the house, found a good sized stone from a rock garden and hefted it as he gauged the distance to a cellar window. Eyes riveted on his watch, he waited until the zero moment and then hurled the rock.

Silk's stone smashed through a big bay window at almost the exact instant. Butch was half a second late, but he wrecked another window. The lights in the house winked out simultaneously, indicating they were all hooked to a main switch conveniently located upstairs.

The Black Bat raced to the window he'd broken, hesitated a bare second and then knew the men inside were heading toward the racket on the first floor. He picked out the larger pieces of glass, unlocked the window and slipped through. The intensely dark cellar meant nothing so far as his eyes were concerned. He moved directly to the cellar steps, raised his automatic and fired a single shot.

The pounding feet on the floor above, all hesitated and then rushed toward the cellarway. Three men rushed down the stairs, guns ready. One had a flashlight and started to spray the darkness with it. A gun blazed. The light went out and its owner slumped to the floor. The other pair started shooting indiscriminately while they retreated. Others were hurrying to aid them. The way probably was clear for Butch and Silk.

A MOMENT or two later this fact was a certainty when the Black Bat heard a howl of anguish and then a tremendous crash as Butch hurled one man against a wall.

The Black Bat opened fire again, with both guns now. He went up those steps rapidly, stopped at the top and listened. There were two quick shots. Someone screamed and a man fell to the floor almost at the Black Bat's feet. Silk was in action now.

The Black Bat catapulted through the doorway, faced a thug who was in the act of taking aim and beat him to the shot by a fraction of a second.

Elsewhere in the house a battle royal raged. The Black Bat found no opposition as he raced upstairs to the second floor and began opening every door to search for Joel King.

He heard a muffled cry, went down along the upper corridor like a flash and another of those cries placed the room from which it originated. He flung the door open.

The Patriot's first lieutenant, Gus, was bending over a bed on which an old man was strapped. Gus had a knife in his hand and it started down.

When the door burst open, Gus whirled, flung the blade at the black robed figure and then drew a gun.

The Black Bat avoided the knife easily. He moved aside just as Gus blazed away. The crook could no longer see a target because of the darkness. He gave a shriek of terror and ran toward the window, got it half open and then, on sudden inspiration, turned toward Joel King again.

His gun leveled, but the finger on the trigger never tightened. Gus died—instantly—with a bullet through the brain.

The Black Bat hurried to the bed, cut the old man loose and found that he was unable to walk.

"You'll have to stay here," he said, "but not for long. There's nothing to be afraid of anymore. I'm the Black Bat."

"Viola—my daughter. She must be here." Joel King grasped the Black Bat's arm. "They'll kill her too."

"Not if I can help it." The Black Bat whirled and streaked for the door. He looked downstairs, saw Butch piling up men in a heap, roaring with every attack he made. The big fellow had thrown aside his gun and resorted to the use of those mighty fists. Silk was doing his part somewhere else in the house. The flat bark of his gun indicated that.

WORKING fast, the Black Bat searched the other rooms on the second floor and located a ladder leading to the attic. He went up this warily, expecting a burst of lead to greet him. There was just silence, darkness and dust. His eyes penetrated the gloom, saw a figure lying in a far corner and he quickly climbed the rest of the way into the attic.

As he started toward the dim figure a man shot from around a chimney. A gun belched death. The Black Bat felt a bullet nick his arm and he flung himself to the floor. Two more slugs whizzed above his head. The killer leaped through the trap door, skidded down the ladder and was gone.

The Black Bat smiled somewhat grimly and went to the figure squirming and tossing in the corner.

Carol was near the back door, biting her nails in anxiety when the Black Bat appeared. He was carrying someone. He whispered instructions to Carol and then plunged back into the house where the sounds of fighting were abating.

Butch had cornered two men who were yowling for mercy. Neither held a gun for that was suicide and they knew it—from having watched Butch tackle others who tried to gun him down. Butch grabbed each man by the neck, dragged them into the middle of the floor and suddenly both were being swung through the air. Their heads collided. Butch let go and they dropped flat.

Butch rubbed his hands and looked for more prey.

Silk came in, smoking gun in his fist. "There were eight or nine of them, sir. One got clear, I'm afraid. Went through the front door while I was busy with two more of them. I don't believe any others made their escape."

"Good," the Black Bat said. "Now let's get out of here before the police arrive and delay us. Carol took the car—it was very necessary—so Silk, you go to the garage behind the house and see if you can get another. Hurry!"

SILK found an expensive sedan, drove it to the door and Butch and the Black Bat piled in. They left the driveway and were rolling south when police cars careened around corners toward the estate.

"Drive to Kurt Miller's place," the Black Bat ordered.

When Silk pulled up, half a block from Kurt Miller's house, the Black Bat looked around, saw no one and disappeared in the alley beside the remains of Miller's burned out tenement house. He reached Miller's rear door, opened it without much trouble and very quietly moved toward the front of the house.

Kurt Miller was pacing the living room floor. He heard a sibilant hiss, froze in his tracks and let one hand rest on a gun butt.

"It is—the Patriot?" he asked.

"Who else?" the Black Bat hissed. "You expected me, didn't you?"

Miller let go of the gun. "Well yes—in a way. I thought you would send one of your men. I . . ." he started toward the door.

"Stop where you are," the Black Bat ordered. "I can't afford to let you see me. We have business. Let's get it over with."

Miller gave a loud gasp of pleasure, ran to his safe and opened it. He drew out several thick sheafs of United States Currency.

"You understand, my friend, this is just a down payment, but you will at once turn the instrument or its blue prints over to me—yes? At least enough so I am sure I am not being cheated. Cheated did I say? forgive me. I have been convinced for days. You have proven the worth of your invention."

"Put the money on the floor," the Black Bat said. "You'll get what you pay for, don't worry."

Miller obeyed, stepped back and rubbed his hands briskly. The huge smile on his face died away suddenly for he saw the grim outlines of the Black Bat facing him. Miller made a grab for his gun, but a hand with steel fingers grasped his wrist. Miller began to whimper.

"Your days as a secret agent are over," the Black Bat told him firmly. "I let you go once before because I thought you might put me on the trail of the Patriot. Now that isn't necessary; but you are going to be put into a cell."

"No—no—" Miller squealed. Then a fist hit him. Miller dropped like a log.

The Black Bat spent a few moments binding the man and locking him in a closet. Scooping up the money the spy had set aside, he rushed out of the house, reached the car and piled in.

"Where to now?" Silk queried.

"Viola King's place, as fast as you can make it. Butch—this stuff I'm putting in your hands is good old United States Currency. Miller was going to pay it over to the Patriot, but I got there first. I don't know how much it represents, but you and Silk are to visit the widow of that printer who was killed. She is to be pensioned off with Miller's money—which isn't such a bad idea at that. Then both of you are to return to the house and wait for me."

CHAPTER XIX

The Huge Fraud

ENTERING swiftly, Commissioner Warner, Captain McGrath and a number of G-Men surprised Viola King at her house.

"We don't know what it's all about yet," Warner told her. "Just let us wait, please. I'm expecting some other men."

Halton and Lockwood showed up five minutes later, just as confused as the others. They all entered the living room. Warner went to a rear window and raised it high. Then he sat down.

Someone was moving at the back of the house. Hank Standish, looking a bit sheepish, came in.

"I—suppose you think it rather odd that I didn't show up before, but the fact is—I didn't know just who you were. Viola asked me to remain here and protect her."

Viola went to his side. "There is nothing to fear from these men, darling."

"That," a voice announced from somewhere behind them, "is the truth."

Everyone turned quickly. The Black Bat stood just inside the open window.

"But," he went on, "one man here is to be feared because he has proved himself extremely dangerous. The Patriot is finished, gentlemen. A spy named Miller was prepared to buy the instrument of death which the Patriot offered for sale. Miller is at the moment, tied up and locked in the closet of his home. One of you federal men will phone your office and have him picked up at once."

"But the Acme Building." Captain McGrath started forward and then checked himself because there was a gun in the Black Bat's fist now. "We should be there now."

"The Acme Building is safe," the Black Bat said. "When you promptly searched it and prevented anyone from entering, you saved the building, Captain."

"What do you mean?" Halton demanded.

"Merely that there will be no further explosions. Mr. Halton—you have unwittingly furthered the efforts of the Patriot. I hope that from this affair you will learn that the police are capable of handling their own job. And you—Mr. Lockwood—were forever present when Halton went about. Why did you never leave him out of your sight?"

Lockwood licked his lips. "I—well —I'm a business man. Halton is a Congressman and I've been trying to get certain things through. I—helped him financially by purchasing some of his holdings. I—just wanted to be sure he wouldn't doublecross me. Then I became interested in this affair and—I just tagged along. Sometimes I even thought Halton was behind this and I wanted to watch him for that reason too."

"Black Bat," McGrath called out. "Who is the Patriot? I know he must be someone present in this room because you had us gather here to see him revealed. What's happened to Joel King?"

"Yes," Viola cried. "Please—is he all right."

"Perfectly well—in fact he happens to be standing in the doorway right now."

Everyone looked in that direction. Joel King, with a pale, frightened girl at his side, took a couple of steps into the room. Suddenly Viola screamed and Hank Standish had a gun in his hand. With an oath he whirled toward the Black Bat. There was one shot — from Captain McGrath's service pistol—and Standish let go of his gun with bloody fingers.

"Thank you, Captain," the Black Bat said. "I noticed you were prepared for trouble, so I held my fire. Yes—Standish is the Patriot. Viola—the one we knew—is his accomplice. She took the place of the real Viola King who had been kidnaped when she was on her way home from school. Joel King rarely permitted his daughter to return home so the false Viola easily slipped into her place without arousing any attention. Joel King was, of course, also kidnaped."

Hank Standish glared at the Black Bat. "All right," he warned, "you've got me, but everyone here is going to die unless I'm permitted to leave here alone. The lethal machine is installed and ready to work. It will wipe all of us out unless you do as I say."

The Black Bat laughed. "Your fraud has stopped working, Standish. In fact so far as I was concerned, it stopped long ago. You have no death machine to explode things at will. The photography planes were sabotaged—by having an extremely explosive chemical placed in the cameras. The explosion was set to synchronize with the flares that were dropped.

"The speed boats were also prepared to blow up with time bombs contained in the speedometers installed after the craft were searched. You set up a machine, yes, but it was as phony as you. Everyone believed I was killed in the blast at that house on the river cliff. One of your men placed bombs in there—the machine was turned on for effect because you knew someone would see it.

"Viola, the false one, posing as Joel King's daughter built up the necessary publicity about the lethal machine. She said it did exist—told her story to anybody who would listen, I suppose.

"Along with your campaign of terror, you made the nation believe you possessed such an instrument. Even Miller fell for it, which, of course, you intended all along. You even set up a hideout in one of his apartments so he'd be sure to contact you."

McGRATH asked. "But what about the man who was blown to bits at the airfield?"

"He was a printer, kidnaped to do the Patriot's printing work on those leaflets. He was permitted to escape and the taxi driver who drove him to the airport was one of the Patriot's men. You'll find him at Police Headquarters when you return. This driver had to help the printer from his car because the man was hurt. During the process, he slipped one of those small but high powered bombs into his pocket. There was no lethal machine and there never will be.

"Now, gentlemen, you have your man—an expert in propaganda. His band of crooks distributed the phonograph records, the fake newspapers, dropped leaflets from building roofs and because Standish was involved in the motion picture business it was not hard for him to arrange, through his men, for certain projectionists to be bribed so they'd slip the section of propaganda film into the regular news reels."

Halton gave a long sigh and sat down heavily. He was mopping his brow when the Black Bat called to him.

"Halton, you were in this house when Joel King was forcibly brought here to open his safe. That was just a ruse to build up the fact that he was working willingly for the Patriot. You were assaulted by the Patriot's men. Can you tell me why?"

"Sure," Halton said. "When they came in, I grabbed a vase and tried to crown one of them. We had a scrap, the vase went through the window and then—well that's all I remember."

"Exactly," the Black Bat said. "I arrived very shortly after. Standish had been tied up by his own men but not hurt. Viola was very tenderly cared for, too. Standish told me he knocked the vase through the window, but—the man was firmly tied. There was no table near the window so how could he pick up a vase and use it?

"I suspected him then, but not the false Viola. She's a clever, resourceful crook. You'll find the money paid to her in this house. It was never transferred to the hearse. One of those you stopped made the contact, but naturally falsified the transfer of those packages to it.

"Which reminds me—the Patriot has a number of crooks working for him. Some are in strategic defense positions. Ferret them out quickly. It should not be difficult if you keep his arrest a secret. I . . . look—the real Viola King is more ill than I thought. Help her!"

By the time Viola King was placed on a davenport, the Black Bat was gone!

BUTCH, Silk and Carol were in Tony Quinn's lab when he returned. While he changed to Tony Quinn's more comfortable tweeds, he told them just what happened.

"And you knew there wasn't a lethal machine." Silk heaved a long sigh. "I wish I'd known it because I never worried so much over anything in my life. You would have had your doubts too—if you were with Carol when they started blasting the golf course all around us."

Quinn laughed. "That gave me my first inkling of the truth. If a lethal machine capable of contacting three fast moving planes high in the sky and during a complete blackout, couldn't pick you and Carol off as you ran across an open golf course in moonlight—well—it made me wonder.

"The golf course simply was mined. They intended to use it on someone to give the illusion that a death ray was at work. Building up that idea was the Patriot's greatest task. It was propaganda, pure and simple."

Carol inquired. "And you suspected Standish all along?"

"Good heavens no. I'd have stopped him long ago if I had any evidence. I got to him partly by a process of elimination. When the Patriot was very busy, Halton and Lockwood were in Washington doing their best to convince other statesmen to pay off. Halton really was sincere. Of course, if such an instrument did exist, twenty million was a small price to pay for it.

"You'll notice Washington didn't do much hesitating. But Standish realized the sum was terrific so, in order to at least get something, he requested a token payment and if the thing still looked safe later on, he'd demand more.

"Standish phoned the fake Viola to build up the machine's reputation even more. They knew G-Men had tapped the wires. In fact Viola went out of her way to let them get into the house. Standish made the call from Halton's summer home. That I knew by checking the call. I saw two men leave the house—with the help of my eyes that can see through darkness. I didn't recognize either of them, but they were fairly big men and Joel King was slight of build. Also I knew Gus was with the Patriot and would naturally leave with him when the shooting started on the beach.

"Therefore I was sure Joel King hadn't been at the summer house and —either the Patriot called Viola or Gus did. When she swore it was her father, I knew she lied. Standish was pretending to be her fiance, even faked a fight with her when she consented to help the Patriot. It was all an act. If Viola were involved, I knew Standish would be too. I . . . someone is coming to the house. Silk—get busy."

Captain McGrath came in after the secret door to the lab was shut, walked up to where Tony Quinn sat, staring into space with sightless eyes.

McGrath said, "Mr. Quinn, I came to apologize. You aren't the Black

Bat. I'm sure of it. We unmasked the Patriot, solved the whole case. That is—ah—the Black Bat did most of it. But—you remember Steve Cobb, the taxi driver who you hired? He's pinched too."

"Steve?" Quinn asked in a surprised voice. "Good heavens, what for?"

"He was one of the Patriot's men assigned to watch you because Viola—who was a fake—also used you to spread propaganda about the lethal machine which also doesn't exist. The. . . ."

"Hold on," Quinn squirmed around in his chair. "This is all very strange to me. Steve Cobb an agent of the Patriot. I can't believe you."

"Yeah—Steve is even boasting about how he fooled you. Now the way I look at it, if you were the Black Bat, you'd have know about it in one minute flat. Steve met the Black Bat all right, while you were right here at home. The Patriot moved into one of those big mansions on Riverside Drive—just took it over while the owner was away. We caught Steve there. I just thought you'd like to know I'd changed my mind. The Black Bat would never have let Steve get away with that."

"My, my," Quinn said. He grinned broadly as McGrath hurried out.

Captain McGrath really believed he'd done a fine piece of work in admitting to Tony Quinn that he wasn't the Black Bat. He kept priding himself on the idea until—as he entered Police Headquarters—someone laughed raucously.

"Say, Captain—I see you've been around the Black Bat again. There's about five of his stickers pasted on your shoulders."

Captain McGrath slammed the door of his office so hard the glass rattled. Captain McGrath was not sure anymore. Then he chuckled. That was really the way he wanted it.

Suddenly Hannah's gun barked at me

SNATCHERS ARE SUCKERS

By ROBERT C. DONOHUE

Author of "Last Race for Geary," etc.

Chauffeur Casey Wades Through a Vicious Kidnap Ring and Lets His Yellow Boss Cop the Glory—but Does All Right for Himself, Too!

I, DENNIS CORNELIUS CASEY, am not the brightest guy in the world but I can take a hint when it hits me between the eyes like a caveman's club. So when a surly growl answered me through the cracked door, saying, "Scram, fella! There's no p h o n e here!" and the door slammed in my face, I went right back to Mortimer.

"They have no phone, sir," I announced.

Mortimer was annoyed. Mortimer was almost always annoyed. I think he was born that way—annoyed because the silver spoon in his mouth wasn't platinum. His old man runs a flock of newspapers and Mortimer is a big shot in the enterprise. But the old man does all the work. Mortimer spends the money.

"Nonsense!" he snapped with that superior tone of his.

For two years, I had been his chauffeur, and for two years I had resisted the urge to poke his elegant puss every time he gave out with his superior, annoyed "Nonsense!" I told myself that a moment's ecstasy wasn't worth a steady thirty bucks a week.

"They *must* have a phone," said Mortimer. "See the wires?"

I saw the wires. They were just visible against the darkening sky. Night was coming in a hurry. The lonely gray road disappeared into purplish haze at both ends. Sandy scrub land to the west glowed faintly under a smoky sunset. The ocean was on the east—nothing but the ocean, half-swallowed in the murk of dusk.

It was a heckuva spot for the car to quit, but that's how it is with these expensive foreign jobs. They're not at all considerate like a Lincoln or a Cadillac, which can be depended upon to break down near a garage—at least within airplane distance of some spare parts that will fit.

"Maybe their phone is not connected," I ventured.

"Nonsense!" said Mortimer. "You just didn't know how to ask them. I'll do it myself!" He threw an annoyed glance at the big, useless car and me and started for the shack.

IT was a crummy little place. You wouldn't think the tenants could afford a telephone. The shack was all alone—there wasn't another building for miles. It was located halfway between the road and the water. To reach it, you had to tightrope a narrow plank across the roadside ditch.

Mortimer negotiated the plank with me steadying the end of it. We stopped and studied the shack.

I didn't like it. In the dimness of fading daylight the scabby window shutters looked sinister.

"Do you hear anything?" whispered Mortimer.

"No. Very quiet folks. No lights, either. I think they are watching us from behind those shutters."

Mortimer started to say, "Nonsense!" but the sudden, incongruous jangle of a telephone startled us both. Light immediately filtered through the shutters, and the ringing was cut off as the receiver was lifted.

"See!" said Mortimer. "There's nothing wrong with that phone!"

I shrugged.

"I still think we ought to wait on the road for a car to come along. There's something phony about this place. The man gave me the impression that—"

"Nonsense!" interrupted Mortimer. He walked across the rickety porch and knocked loudly on the door. He seemed very brave, but I knew he wasn't, because, when nobody answered his first knock, he beckoned me closer before he knocked again.

Finally, the door cracked open as it had for me.

"Whaddaya' want?" snarled that heavy, ugly voice.

"I would like to use your telephone for just a moment," said Mortimer, unabashed by the apparent hostility. "My car has broken down. I'd like to call a garage in the next town."

"Wait a minute."

The door closed. Mortimer looked at me. I shrugged. The door opened wide, and a man and a woman stared out at us.

I couldn't see their faces clearly because the light was behind them. The man was long and lanky. The woman was tall too. She had a loose mop of yellow hair.

"Okay," growled the man. "Come in and phone, but make it snappy!"

"Thanks," murmured Mortimer, stepping past them into the room. I eased in also, before the guy could close the door. I would rather have stayed outside, but I was supposed to be a bodyguard as well as a chauffeur.

THE room was just what I expected — dirty and barely furnished. A rickety table held a new pack of playing cards, a half-bottle of bourbon and a couple of glasses. An old, brass-poster bed shared the remaining space with a frayed davenport.

On the davenport was what, at first glance, I thought was only a heap of blankets. But as Mortimer walked across the room to the telephone, the blankets moved, and I heard a moan. Mortimer stopped.

"That's my sister!" said the gal with the frowzy yellow hair. "She's sick!"

"Oh!" Mortimer glanced curiously at the blankets as he picked up the phone.

The couple watched Mortimer, and I watched the couple. The man's lean face needed a shave, except for a two-inch crescent on his right cheek where an old scar showed white in the middle of black beard. His stringy hair was oily and uncombed. His eyes were like dull black marbles. He fished out a pack of cigarettes, selected and lit one and never took those eyes off Mortimer.

The woman glanced my way a couple of times. She was almost as frayed-looking as the davenport. She was skinny. Too much cheap rouge emphasized the boniness of her coarse face. She might have been pretty, ten years ago.

Mortimer got Information, Information got Mortimer a number and Mortimer finally got a garage. As soon as the call was finished, the guy held open the door.

"Wait outside," he said.

"Of course," assented Mortimer. "Thanks for the use of your phone, old man." He went through his pockets for change.

"That's okay," said the guy impatiently. "You don't owe me anything." The bony blonde flicked nervous blue eyes at the davenport.

Again there was a weak moan. The blankets moved. A corner fell away, and I got a glimpse of auburn hair and a pretty face. The blonde hurried to the davenport. I grabbed Mortimer's arm.

"Let's go," I urged, trying to sound casual.

But Mortimer had seen that face, too. He was too shocked to pretend he hadn't.

"Barbara!" he gasped. *Barbara Stevens!*"

The guy with the scar slammed the door and pulled out an automatic at the same time.

"What's Miss Stevens doing here?" demanded Mortimer of the blonde.

"I insist—"

The guy shoved his gun against Mortimer's ribs, and Mortimer closed his mouth abruptly to keep his heart from jumping out.

"Never mind about Barbara," grated the guy. "You can start worrying about yourself! Who are you? How come you know her?"

Mortimer wasn't annoyed now. He was scared stiff, fingertips pointing at the low ceiling.

"I'm Mortimer Allenby," he gulped. "I know Barbara Stevens through her family. Same beach club. What are you—"

THE guy pushed Mortimer into a chair. He waved the gun at me, and I, too, grabbed a seat.

"Didn't you clucks know she was snatched yesterday?" asked Scarface.

We shook our heads. The guy raised an incredulous eyebrow.

"We've been on a fishing trip," explained Mortimer as if he were afraid the gun would pop if he didn't make everything clear. "The radio was out of order, and we haven't seen a paper since we left the boat."

"When did you leave the boat?"

"An hour ago."

"Where?"

"At my cottage north of Bellport."

"Where were you going?"

"To New York, until the car stopped and this happened.

"What—?"

"Were you expected any place tonight?"

"No."

"How come you were off the main highway?"

Mortimer looked imploringly at me.

"I wanted to make time," I said. "There's hardly any traffic on this coast road. No trucks."

Scarface strolled to the davenport, keeping the gun aimed at me and my boss. I heard the blonde say, "Quiet all day—only move out of her—had to happen now!"

The guy shrugged and handed the cannon to the blonde. She kept us covered while he picked up the phone and murmured a number. He held that black-marble stare on Mortimer.

"Yeah, Midge, this is Lou again. . . . No, I didn't forget anything. . . . No, don't worry, Midge. Maybe this is good. A punk and his chauffeur just dropped in. The punk's name is Mortimer Allenby—droopy looking twerp, sandy hair, little red mustache, talks with a kind of a English accent. . . . Oh, you know him! . . . Newspapers? That's no good, eh? Shall I bump 'em? . . . I dunno. Wait a minute."

He scowled disgustedly at Mortimer for a moment.

"Allenby, do you think your old man would pay fifty grand to get you back alive?"

"Of course he would!" I butted in. Mortimer nodded vigorously.

"Yeah," said Lou into the phone, "Okay, you'll send it right away. Anything new on the girl? . . . Okay, but she's a cute kid just the same. . . . Okay, okay, I'll do it. See you there later."

He gently replaced the receiver.

"We're leaving," he announced. "Going on a little boat trip."

"What about my car?" asked Mortimer.

"That's why we're leaving."

Lou stepped to the bed, reached under a pillow and pulled out another automatic. Now he and his girl-friend each had a gun.

I wouldn't have tried anything even if Mortimer hadn't been too scared to help.

The blonde waved hers at me.

"Okay, big boy," she said in a flinty monotone. "You got muscles. You can carry the debutante."

"It's an honor," I said.

"Don't try to be funny," growled Lou.

Barbara was apparently drugged, her pert face strangely white. I hoped they hadn't given her too much.

I MOVED the ragged blankets. Bright beach pajamas covered the sleeping beauty. Carefully, I slid my arms under her.

"Pick 'er up! Pick 'er up!" rasped the blonde. "She won't break!"

Barbara didn't weigh more than a hundred fifteen, but she was limp and awkward to handle. A man, I would have hoisted over my shoulder. Her head rolled disturbingly when I lifted her.

"Where do we go?" I snapped at Lou.

"Take it easy, flunkey!" Lou snapped back. "Follow Hannah."

The bony blonde who was called Hannah led us outside through the rear door. It was quite dark now— a black night with no moon. There was the smell of the sea and the soft thud of surf on the sheltered beach.

A low ramshackle pier stretched a hundred feet over the water.

"Watch where you walk," ordered Lou from the rear. "Some boards are missing."

He lit a flashlight, but it didn't help

me because my burden prevented me from seeing where my feet were stepping.

But I made it to the end of the pier. We all did. Lou's light picked out a mahogany-hulled speedboat. He prodded Mortimer.

"You hop in first."

Mortimer hopped in.

"Now hand the girl to him," Lou ordered.

"I can make it," I said. And I stepped down into the bobbing boat without relinquishing Barbara.

"All right," growled Lou. "But next time I tell you to do something, you do it my way. Understand?"

"Sure. I'm just trying to be helpful."

"Your'e trying to be funny, and it's gonna get you in trouble."

Lou cast off the lines. He and Hannah got into the front seat. She faced aft, pointing her gun at us over the motor hatch cover. The starter whined. The motor coughed and roared. Lou headed the boat out to sea.

UNDER different circumstances, I could have enjoyed that ride. The throbbing motor lifted the boat high. Spray was a white spinning wall, and occasional drops flew against my face.

The bundle I tenderly embraced was no longer limp. Barbara was conscious. I knew it when I carried her from the shack into darkness.

Now, her lips were against my ear; her quick breath tickled my eardrums.

"Hello, Dennis," she murmured.

"Hello, Miss Barbara. I didn't hand you over to Mortimer. I was afraid he'd drop you."

"Thanks. You're safer, Dennis."

I took time out to grin. Barbara had once dated my boss. He had made a pass at her—to his immediate regret. I wondered if that was what she meant.

"How long have you been awake?"

"Long time. I've been faking. They grabbed me yesterday morning, forced me into a car and gave me the needle. I woke up last night in the shack, and they fed me a doped drink, but I managed to ditch most of it. All today, I kept my eyes closed and listened."

"Smart girl!"

"I heard plenty, but what good will it do? They're going to kill me tonight!" She said it without even a tremor in her voice. Barbara was no sissy.

Next to me, Mortimer was shivering, too scared to open his mouth.

"Miss Barbara," I said. "They won't kill you. Don't worry."

"If dad can't raise the money tonight, they will."

"He'll raise it."

"Dad's practically broke. Nobody knew. He can't raise much."

"Don't worry. This party's only beginning. Keep faking. We'll surprise 'em when the right time comes."

Lou seemed to know where he was going; I figured he was steering by the stars. Soon he cut the motor, and the boat idled to a low dark blot of an island. Barbara and I stopped talking.

"Where are we?" blurted Mortimer.

"Shut up!" hissed Hannah.

The boat bumped gently against a small, makeshift dock. Lou scrambled out and hitched the lines.

"All out!" he ordered. "End of the line."

"I don't like that 'end of the line' stuff," I muttered.

It was only a few uneven steps from the crude dock to an equally makeshift hut. Hannah went in first and lit a kerosene lamp. The yellow light threw eerie shadows on driftwood walls. The room was damp and smelled of decay. A shabby couch occupied the far wall. As I carried Barbara to it, the floor's rotten wood crumbled under my feet.

"Now I'm gonna tie you two guys up," announced Lou.

"That's okay by me," I said. "Then maybe you and Hannah can put away those cannons; they make me nervous."

"Me, too," piped Mortimer unexpectedly.

HANNAH produced some rope from a closet in a corner. Then she held a gun on us while Lou tied our wrists and ankles to chairs. He took his time and made a tight job of it.

My only consolation was that I had picked out a chair that was close to Barbara's couch. She could untie me if she got a chance.

Lou stood back and admired his job. He turned to Barbara. "Hannah," he said. "Shouldn't this dame be awake by now?"

"Yeah, I think so."

"Maybe we better tie her, too."

"No, you don't have to. She'll be too sick from all that dope to make any trouble." Hannah shook Barbara roughly, and the auburn head rolled as if it were on a string. What an act!

"You think we gave her too much?" asked Lou. He didn't seem worried about it. "You think maybe she won't wake up anymore, huh?"

"Geez! I don't know!" Hannah answered irritably. "Maybe she won't. I'm no doctor!"

"All right, don't get sore!" Lou walked to the door. "I'm gonna watch for Midge's signal."

For a while, there wasn't a sound. Hannah sat on the edge of the couch and stared at Barbara. I was afraid that Barbara might open an eye to see what was what and Hannah would find out she was faking, so I tried to draw the big blonde's attention away from her.

"How much are you getting for the girl?" I asked.

"Shut up!" snarled Hannah.

"You're a sweet kid," I countered.

"If you don't shut your mouth, I'll put a gag in it!"

"Aw, Hannah! Why be tough with me? I've got no hard feelings. Tonight isn't costing me anything. I don't care how much you get out of Allenby and the girl so long as I don't wind up in the drink."

"That's just where you will wind up," maliciously g r a t e d Hannah. "You're not worth anything. Just a nuisance!"

"I resent that! I've tried to be helpful. Didn't I lug the girl to the boat and from the boat? And didn't I sit nice and quiet while our pal Lou roped me to this chair?"

"Sure, sure. With a gun in your back you were fine."

"Without a gun I'd be just as cooperative. Untie me, and I'll prove it."

A sour chuckle sifted between Hannah's thin red lips. It was strange how the soft yellow kerosene light took the hardness out of her face. The queer chuckle broke off, and she looked unhappy.

"This isn't funny," she said. "I'm sorry for you, big boy. When Midge comes over—after all, you're a witness. They'll use you and the girl, too, if Stevens doesn't produce—as an example to scare quick money out of Allenby. Yeah, I'm sorry for you, big boy."

"And I'm sorry for you, Hannah. You're not kidding me with your hardboiled act. I can see a lot in your face and in your eyes. You don't belong in this dirty game. You were never meant to—"

"Aw, cut the corn!" snapped Hannah. She moved jerkily from the couch and walked to the door. She stood there, watching Lou, on the dock.

A FAINT creak sounded behind me as Barbara shifted slightly. I felt her tugging at the rope around my wrists. If her dainty hands loosened those knots, it would be first cousin to a miracle. I didn't have much hope.

Hannah seemed very interested in whatever was happening outside. She didn't turn even when the old couch creaked again as Barbara tried my ankles. My wrists were bound as tightly as ever. The knots were too tough.

Suddenly, the pressure of the rope on my ankles relaxed. I stared at the back of Hannah's blonde head and kept whispering softly.

"Don't turn around! Don't turn around! Don't turn around!"

At a time like that, you grab at anything—even mental telepathy, which you ordinarily figure is so much hooey.

Barbara was again tearing at my wrist bindings. It must have been tough on her tender fingers, but she worked frantically.

Outside, Lou made a noise that sounded like a grunt. I could see the faint reflection of his light winking off and on. Hannah straightened, then walked outside and joined Lou on the dock. Now Barbara really went to work. I heard a fingernail snap, and a whispered exclamation that was unladylike, but excusable under the circumstances. All at once, my hands were free.

It was none too soon, either.

"Here they come!" Mortimer whispered, and a second later, Lou and Hannah were back. They looked extra glum.

"What's wrong?" I asked, hoping they wouldn't notice my loosened bindings.

Lou didn't even look at me.

"The girl's old man didn't come through," said Hannah.

Lou's weird eyes were fixed on Barbara.

"It's a shame," he muttered. "She's a cute kid."

The blonde looked a little frightened.

"How do you know he didn't come through?" I asked.

"Midge just told us—by flashlight from the shore."

"Maybe Midge is double-crossing you—scramming with the dough while you stick on this island."

Hannah shot an uncertain glance at Lou. Lou shook his head.

"Midge is on his way," he said. "He'll be here in an hour."

So we had an hour. We waited in silence. The lamp's dirty yellow light flickered against the brown walls and beat vainly against the blackness of the open doorway. I wondered halfheartedly whether a passing boat, police or coast-guard, might notice the

faint light and investigate. But there didn't seem to be any passing boats. The silence grew heavy.

The blonde had been standing at the door. Finally, she came over to the couch. I could see her gun weighing down the pocket of her light jacket as she walked. She bent over Barbara.

"That kid will never come out of it," I said. "You've killed her! Every minute you hang around here makes it more likely you'll get caught. You'll burn for that. Kidnapping's bad enough, but for murder, you burn!"

"Shut up!" hissed Hannah. She went back to the door, glanced around, then walked out to the dock. I heard her high heels clumping back and forth.

Lou was nervous too. He smoked cigarettes chain fashion and paced the hut's rotten floor. The butt of his automatic, peeping from his hip pocket, gleamed dully.

THE hour was almost gone. Now was the time to make the break— before Midge arrived, and while the blonde was outside. But Lou would plug me as soon as I moved from my chair. I had to get him near me— where I could reach him without warning.

"Lou, gimme a cigarette," I begged.

"Shut up!"

I tried another angle.

"Lou," I mocked, "you're a sucker!" Funny how every crook would rather be called anything than a sucker. Lou stopped, glared at me, then went back to his pacing and smoking.

"You're a sucker, Lou. Your pal has run out on you with the Stevens dough. And while you're wasting time here he's probably collecting from old man Allenby, too. You're a

walking, looking at me with his black-marble eyes.

I grinned at him, timed his steps, and murmured, "Sucker!" He heard it twice every time he crossed the room. In a minute, he was sick of it. He came over to me.

"I told you to shut up!" he snarled. He walloped me across the jaw with the hard palm of his big hand. I let him hit me once. Then I leaped from the chair.

My head butted his face. I felt the shock, even through my thick Irish skull, so I guess it didn't do Lou any good. Instinctively, he reached for his gun, but he never touched it because I bent him then with a left in the stomach. I corrected his posture with a hefty uppercut, then battered him across the room with every shot in the locker.

The wall stopped him, and the hut shook. I pinned him there and drove my right into his bloody face.

"Never give a rat a break," is my motto. Suddenly, Hannah was standing in the doorway, her automatic barking at me.

I let go of Lou and lifted my hand. Lou slowly slid down into a loose heap, his head bumping the rough wall.

"Put up your hands!" shouted Hannah.

"I got 'em up!" I observed weakly. She'd missed me when I was moving after Lou, but I'd be crazy to play my luck too far.

Hannah glanced anxiously at what was left of Lou. She gritted her teeth and glared at me.

"If you killed him, I'll kill you!" she said.

Believe me, the gal wasn't fooling. I kept my hands high.

"He's okay," I said. "Just tired. Well, what now? You're boss. I wasn't fast enough."

Hannah didn't seem quite sure what to do. She darted a suspicious scowl at Barbara who still pretended to be asleep, but the gun held an unwavering bead on my middle. My arms were getting tired when the drone of an approaching boat reached us, and every breath stopped for a shocked second.

"That's Midge!" cried Hannah. "*He'll* handle you!"

I didn't doubt it. Now, I'd be tied again. It seemed as if I'd skinned my knuckles on Lou's wire beard for nothing.

Lou groaned. He was huddled grotesquely. I thought of the gun in his pocket. "I'd better straighten him out," I suggested. "He can't breathe so well like this."

"Go ahead," nodded Hannah. Her eyes narrowed. "But keep away from his gun!"

I SLIPPED my hands under his armpits and lifted. Hannah circled into the room so that I wouldn't be able to use Lou as a shield. She was smart, but she didn't figure on Barbara. As soon as Hannah's back was turned, Barbara came to life and threw a pillow.

It glanced off the frowzy head. I ducked under the gun, grabbed Hannah's skinny wrist and twisted. The automatic spat harmlessly at the wall. Hannah screamed with pain. Her fingers stiffened, and the gun dropped. I kicked it toward Barbara.

All at once, everything was quiet, except for the roar of Midge's boat— going away! I chuckled.

"Your pal's running out on you after all! The noise scared the rat!"

Hannah slumped into a chair, sobbing—no fight left.

The ride back to the mainland was pleasant with Barbara snuggled close. Mortimer bravely kept the two guns aimed at sobbing Hannah and battered Lou.

That's the way he posed for the pictures that were wired all over the country. Maybe Mortimer's importance in the business had something to do with it. Anyhow, the papers made him a national hero. The stories skipped the fact that he had been only a spectator while the action was popping.

All of which was okay by Barbara and me. Reporters have to play politics once in a while just like everyone else. Usually, newspapers tell things right.

Soon, they'll be telling you about the wedding of an ex-debutante and an ex-chauffeur.

"We'll wait—if it takes a week—for Grogan's ghost to come"

A GRAVE FOR GROGAN
By NORMAN A. DANIELS
Author of "It Comes Out Murder," "The Mailed Fist," etc.

Detective Kennedy Had to Find the Killers So That Grogan's Restless Ghost Could Rest in Its Own Tomb!

ETECTIVE - LIEUTENANT PAT KENNEDY wasn't an acrobat, but he certainly looked like one as he swung from a rope and guided himself down the sheer side of a brick wall. Foot by foot he descended, his objective a window ten stories above the ground.

Once this building had been a theater, but enterprising promoters had turned it into a night club with a few hidden rooms that served as gambling dens. The place was equipped with all kinds of protective devices to announce the orthodox coming of an intruder.

Somewhere inside the building were two dangerous killers, men who hated police officers with the intensity bred over long years of fighting them.

Kennedy knew the danger he faced, but it added to his determination to take the men—dead or alive. He slid down the rope another notch and his toes touched the window sill.

He clung to the rope with one hand,

used the other in an attempt to raise the window, and swore softly when it refused to move. He drew a knife, opened the blade with his teeth, maneuvered it expertly, and the latch was forced back.

A moment later he was inside. Kennedy snapped on his flash, avoided a cheap desk and a couple of chairs. He opened the door, listened, and when he heard nothing, stepped into the hallway.

Tony Judel and Joe Varno were holed-up in here. It wasn't the first time that this place had been used as a cooling-off spot for men with the heat on them. Kennedy mopped sweat with his handkerchief and drew his hip holstered gun. He spun the cylinder experimentally and then moved in the direction of a door beneath which a stream of yellow light shone.

He listened outside the door for a moment and heard the sound of ice clinking in glasses and the slap-slap of playing cards as they were thrown on a smooth surface. He tightened his grip on the knob, turned it gently until the latch was all the way back. Then he put his foot against the panels and gave the door a mighty kick. Simultaneously he catapulted into the room.

Both men seated at a small table were on their feet instantly. One reached behind him and the lights winked out. Kennedy raised his flashlight, pressed the switch and for a bare second the path of light revealed two thugs, their teeth bared in a snarl of hatred. Then a gun blasted and the flashlight seemed to be picked out of Kennedy's grip by an invisible force.

Kennedy lunged toward the open door. One of the thugs, bent on making a break, met Kennedy head on. Both men were sent reeling back by the impact. Kennedy was the first to recover.

He jumped forward, located the thug with his hands and punched for the crook's chin. He missed and took a glancing blow on the cheek. The thug's fist suddenly was seized in an iron grip. Cursing and yelling to his companion for help, he felt himself yanked forward.

Kennedy hammered a short jab into the pit of his enemy's stomach and drew a sharp grunt of pain as a reward. The thug was doubled up. Kennedy judged the direction of his chin, slapped an experimental jab in that direction and followed it up with a vicious hook. The thug fell backward and landed with a thump that resounded through the huge, empty building.

AS Kennedy turned, the other man leaped on his back. Two strong hands grasped his throat and squeezed hard. Kennedy reached up, secured a grip on the long, disheveled hair of his opponent and pulled. He sent the man upward and over his head to finally crash against the wall four feet distance. Kennedy found a match in his pocket. As the tiny flame cast flickering shadows around the room, he saw that the first crook was reaching for the gun he had dropped.

Kennedy kicked the weapon away, discovered the light switch and turned it on. He whipped out his own gun, smoothed his hair back and pulled a chair into the middle of the room.

"A fine way to welcome a visitor," he said grimly. "Come on, you two— get up!"

The shorter of the pair was Tony Judel, a baby-faced, pink-cheeked killer. Joe Varno was a gangling, six-footer. Both men arose warily and kept their hands shoulder high.

Kennedy indicated a davenport across the room. "Have a seat, boys. This is a social call."

Joe Varno made a wry face.

"Yeah—you just dropped in for tea. We know you, Kennedy. We know why you're here too. You think Tony and me bumped off your pal—Grogan. If we did — you prove it!"

Kennedy restrained an impulse to put his gun away and use his bare fists again. For once in his life, Kennedy almost believed in the third degree. Then he shrugged and relaxed.

"Look, you two," he said grimly. "Grogan and I were friends for twenty years. A month ago Grogan witnessed the holdup of a jewelry store. He didn't have a camera eye, but anyone with even fair eyesight could recognize you two mugs even if you were masked. In fact, he even saw you, Varno, without a mask. In the excitement yours became loose. But Grogan was the witness. Without his testimony, you could laugh off any arrest for robbery and murder. Yes—the clerk in that store died. It's bad for the health of a sixty-eight-year-old man to be slugged on the head with a gun butt."

Tony Judel leaned forward.

"We don't have to listen to this baloney," he snapped. "If you're making a pinch for that job, go ahead and make it. You can't prove anything. You just said Grogan was the only man who could convict us."

"Sure of yourself, aren't you?" Kennedy said. "You know that Grogan is dead. Somebody lured him to an isolated section a week ago. He never came back. You two birds did that because it was the only way to save your own skins. You knew Grogan would keep on going until he landed you."

Varno started to get up, but a gesture of Kennedy's gun reseated him on the davenport.

"Okay, copper, you can put the cuffs on me. I don't know what you're talking about and my lawyer will have me out of the coop in two hours."

Kennedy drew his handcuffs, approached the pair cautiously and cuffed Judel's left wrist to Varno's right. Then he sat down again. Both crooks used their free hands to wipe their sweating faces. It was early

autumn and there was a faint chill to the night air outside, but they were perspiring profusely.

"I know I can't convict you of killing Grogan," Kennedy went on, "because nobody saw you kill him, and we have no corpse for evidence. You win—so far—but I've got a little proposition for you. Grogan came of an old Irish family. He was a superstitious soul—believed in ghosts and banshees and the idea that a man's soul can't rest if his body isn't decently buried—in his own grave. Makes you laugh, doesn't it?"

VARNO spat on the floor.

"Listen, copper, we don't know anything about Grogan. We're glad he's dead. I wish every flatfoot in the world was dead—but that don't say we knocked Grogan off. What do you want us to do—give the poor stiff a decent burial?"

Kennedy walked over and stood before them.

"All right—you asked for it. Grogan told me this—that if he died at the hands of murderers, he'd return somehow to tell me who they were. Laugh that off. You don't believe in ghosts. Well, neither do I, but Grogan did and sometimes a man's beliefs transcend the doubts of others. I think Grogan will come back. I think he'll drive you two mad. What are you sweating about if you're not worried? It's not hot in here."

"I'm sick of listening to you talk." Varno snarled. "Take us in. We been pinched before and we always got out. This time ain't no different."

Kennedy looked down at them. He continued talking just as though he'd never been interrupted:

"Grogan worked hard on that jewelry store stick-up and murder. He knew you were the killers and he checked up. He found out that you maintain four different hideouts to hole up in when the heat is on. He planned to raid those places, but you got him first.

"Unfortunately Grogan never told anyone the location of those spots, with the exception of this joint. That's how I found you. Now—Grogan is dead. I know he is. I can feel it—even in here. His body is hidden and his soul is crying out for a decent burial. The corpse is at one of those hideouts. This is your last chance to produce it."

Judel shrugged his shoulders in contempt.

"He's clean off his nut. Maybe we better call a cop to protect us, huh?"

Kennedy reached down, grabbed Judel by the collar and shook him violently.

"You won't laugh long—either of you. I'll find his body. I'll—hey—what's the matter with you guys?"

Both thugs sat stiff as boards, staring past Kennedy. Their faces were slowly draining of color. Judel's lips twitched. Kennedy turned around and gave a loud gasp.

There was a radiator across the room and on the white wall above it were faint, pinkish marks. Like writing being created by some invisible hand. Gradually the marks became brighter and brighter while three men stared with intense awe at the phenomenon.

There were four lines of it. The color of the writing gradually became blood red and then, as if the ink had really been warm blood, the letters ran.

"Grogan!" Kennedy exhaled. "Grogan—his handwriting! Blood! It's written in blood!"

As if some mysterious force impelled him, Kennedy approached the wall. He read the four lines and their meaning was at once clear. The ghostly hand had written four locations—four places which only the dead Grogan and the two terror stricken killers in this room, could possibly know. Kennedy reached up automatically and his finger touched the wall. As he backed away, the words seemed to fade.

Varno jumped up.

"It's a trick! A trick to make us talk!"

Kennedy approached them. He extended his hand and they shrank back at the sight of the crimson stain on his fingers. Very deliberately Kennedy touched Varno's hand. The crook stared down at the wet, warm blood that was smeared across his flesh. He let out a weird wail and fell back on the sofa.

Judel just sat there, staring at the wall like a man entranced. Kennedy looked again. The handwriting had faded into oblivion.

He whirled on his two prisoners.

"So you don't believe, eh? Well, I'll admit that I didn't, either. I was trying to scare you into a confession, but I—I didn't have anything to do with that—that writing on the wall. I wasn't even near the wall. Nobody was! Grogan wrote those words in blood. His own blood that you two hyenas spilled."

"A trick," Varno mumbled. "It was a trick. There ain't no ghosts."

THEN he looked down at his hand again and gulped. There certainly was blood, anyway. It was clotting into a stiff mass. Kennedy jerked both men to their feet and drew his gun.

"We're traveling. This is how Grogan would have wanted it. Get going!"

"Wh-where!" Varno gasped.

"There were four addresses written on the wall by Grogan. It wasn't a trick. Such things can't be faked. Those addresses are the ones I wanted —the ones Grogan alone knew. We're going there. Something tells me Grogan will be there, too. When we reach the right one, he'll give us a sign."

"But-but you can't do that," Varno protested shrilly. "You can't. It's-it's inhuman."

Judel recovered some of his wits.

"Aw—pipe down. I tell you it's a

new kind of third degree. Nobody can tell me there's ghosts — or that Grogan is walking around scaring us. Go ahead, copper, do anything you want. We don't know a thing."

Kennedy marched them downstairs, across the big ballroom and out the door. His car was parked around the corner and he forced them into the front seat. He unlocked one cuff, jerked Varno toward the steering wheel and passed the chain around it. He clapped the other cuff on Judel's wrist. Both thugs were hunched almost on top of one another. Kennedy's hands shook visibly as he reached into the glove compartment for another flashlight.

"Don't tell me you're uncomfortable," he said. "But I hope you are. Now if you try any tricks, you'll be wrecked with the car and me. We're going to that first address Grogan wrote — the house near the public dumping grounds on the outskirts. If you rats buried Grogan, that's as clever a place as any."

Neither of the prisoners replied. Varno still seemed incapable of speech and Judel was bolstering his courage by a constant stream of curses.

Half an hour later Kennedy turned into a rutted road and stopped beside an abandoned house. Smoke and ashes from the burning dump covered everything. Kennedy unlocked one cuff, brought it around the steering post and promptly closed it in place again. He menaced his prisoners with drawn pistol.

"Want to talk?" he asked softly. "Personally—I'm not keen on what I must do. There's no telling what will happen."

"We ain't got anything to talk about," Judel rasped. "You're nuts, copper, and Varno will be the same way pretty soon. But you're on the wrong track. We didn't knock off Grogan."

"Let's go!" Kennedy jabbed Judel's spine with the gun. He forced them to march inside the rickety old house.

Ashes coated the floor, the discarded furniture, the stairs and the banister. They entered the big parlor. Kennedy brushed off a straight-backed chair for himself and straddled it.

Varno and Judel, backed against the wall, were sweating again. Judel's crafty eyes flashed across the floor. If anyone had been in this room within the last two days, footprints would have been visible.

"Wh-what you going to do?" Varno whined. "Keep us here all night?"

"If it's necessary," Kennedy answered. "I don't think it will be. Grogan knows we're here. He'll give us some sign. You boys didn't know him very well—you didn't know how an idea stuck with him. Like the way he wanted to be buried, for instance. That would have followed him in death. You can't deny those words written in blood. This is one of your hideouts, isn't it?"

"I never saw the joint before," Judel snapped.

KENNEDY lighted half-burned candles on the mantel. Varno seemed to perk up as if the light gave him new courage. Judel sneered.

An hour passed without a word being spoken. Kennedy arose from time to time and moved the candles. In a short time they'd be consumed. He looked at the walls closely and then sat down again. The shirts of Varno and Judel were wet, their faces grimy and their eyes shining in fear.

"Grogan!" Kennedy suddenly called out. "Grogan!"

"Stop that!" Varno yelled. "Stop it, you're driving me nuts. I—I can't stand any more of this. I can't stand it, I tell you! I—I—Tony—look! It's that blood again. Grogan's blood!"

Kennedy arose so fast that his chair toppled over. He swiveled and his eyes grew wide. The setting was just the same as it had been in the gambling place. There was a bare wall on the north side of the room. A rusty, ash-covered radiator was set in the middle of it and—just above the radiator—one word gleamed—in blood-red letters.

"No!"

Varno shrieked in terror. Judel struck him across the face savagely.

"Get hold of yourself, sap. The dick is staging this to make you sing."

But Varno's eyes were riveted on the wall. The single word was slowly fading away and at the same time the candles flickered as though a breeze passed before them.

"We'll keep going," Kennedy announced flatly. "We'll visit the next place that Grogan wrote on the wall. If it's not the right one, he'll tell us. No ghosts, eh? Listen—you guys are so scared you can hardly walk, but if I wasn't trying to help Grogan, I'd be just as scared. Outside—and remember there's a gun on you."

Kennedy said nothing as they drove back to town. A storm was raging somewhere in the west and Varno cringed with each flash of lightning. Judel just stared through the windshield.

Kennedy stopped the car beside a huge warehouse on the riverfront. They were still uptown and the sounds of traffic didn't reach this spot. Kennedy walked his prisoners into the warehouse.

At the door, Varno recoiled and began blubbering. Judel hit him again and whispered a warning. Kennedy marched them across the huge, empty floor toward a small office at the back. The warehouse hadn't been used in months. In the office they found a small desk, two chairs and a desk lamp that threw more shadows than light.

"We'll wait," Kennedy said. "If it takes a week—we'll wait. Grogan will come. He's bound to. He's restless. The ghosts of all murdered men are restless. Stand against the wall, you two. I'm going to look around."

Kennedy lifted the metal shade off the desk lamp. He gazed at the four walls thoughtfully and then he gave a grunt. With long, eager steps, he walked over to the farther wall. His fingers ran across it.

"Holes," he said grimly. "Bullet holes—about the height of Grogan's heart. He was killed here! I know it or he wouldn't have led us to this place. You stood him against the wall and blasted out his life."

Varno g r o a n e d dismally. Even Judel seemed affected now. His eyes were bulging and once again the sweat rolled down his face.

"But there should be blood-stains," Kennedy went on. "I don't see any. You washed them off. Then you dragged his body out of here and buried it. Where? Talk, you pair of killers. Talk before Grogan comes back and makes you."

JUDEL seemed to wilt. He said something, but it was so low that Kennedy couldn't distinguish the words. He stepped closer and Judel continued to mumble. Then, suddenly, the killer lunged forward. He had only one free hand, but he managed to smash home a vicious punch to Kennedy's face.

The detective reeled, tripped and fell. Judel gave a howl of glee, yanked Varno with him and leaped on top of the detective. His free hand sought Kennedy's throat and fastened there, leech-like. His knees held the detective prone and Judel kept howling in pleasure.

"Maybe your ghost will come back and haunt us, Kennedy. Maybe you'll write things on the wall to scare us. Anyway, you'll see Grogan. The two of you can have fun haunting me and Varno. Sure—that's it—see if you can scare us."

"Tony — Tony — don't kill him," Varno shrieked. "Don't do it. He'll come back, too. He'll meet Grogan. They'll both come back. Don't kill him. Grogan's ghost is enough."

Judel had a savage answer on his lips, but the words wouldn't come. He was looking across Varno's slumped form. His eyes grew wide and bulged slightly. The murderous fingers around Kennedy's throat relaxed their grip. Varno let out a scream and Judel's own shriek joined in chorus. They got up and retreated, step by step. Judel had one hand thrust out as if to ward off the horror before them.

Kennedy arose slowly, one hand stroking his discolored throat. He saw the same thing that made the killers cringe. There were three bullet holes in the wall. They formed a crude triangle and in their center—drops of blood seemed to sprout out of the wood and slowly drip to the floor. They disappeared behind the steam radiator.

Then—mysteriously—they could be seen again. Drops of blood that gradually formed a straight line toward the door, like blood flowing out of the wounds of a murdered man. Kennedy had his gun out. Judel screamed. Kennedy grabbed his shoulder and forced him to follow the trail of blood that grew visible as they progressed. It led out of the office, across the wide floor and only Kennedy's flashlight revealed it now.

Then Varno collapsed. He sank to his knees for a moment before he toppled over, pulling Judel down with him. Varno's breath came in jerks and his chest heaved like that of a dying man. Judel raised his head. Kennedy was shining the flash ahead, picking out the trail of blood as it formed before their eyes.

"Yes—yes, we killed Grogan," Judel suddenly yelled. "We stood him against the wall. We shot him—both of us. There was blood on the wall. We cleaned it up. We dragged him out—right along the floor where the blood shows. We cleaned that up, too. Make him go away, Kennedy. Make him go! I'll tell you where we hid the body. It's in the river, in a block of cement. We made it look like a wharf piling. Even that wouldn't hold him. Make him stop! I'll go crazy!"

Kennedy drew a long breath. Sud-denly the warehouse was flooded with light. Four detectives swarmed into the place. Judel saw them coming and the terror in his eyes was replaced by fear—not of ghosts—but fear of the electric chair.

"You heard him, boys?" Kennedy asked. "Send the diver down again. He saw that new piling yesterday, but he never suspected Grogan's corpse was inside of it. And thanks for the help."

CAPTAIN BURKE of the Homicide Squad slapped Kennedy across the shoulder.

"I take back whatever I said about this dizzy scheme of yours. It worked, and that's proof you're a smarter man than me. Say—that stuff looked great, didn't it?"

Judel strained forward, pulling Varno's still unconscious form with him.

"You mean that blood in the wall was phony? That Grogan ain't got no ghost?"

"About the ghost, I wouldn't say," Kennedy smiled. "The blood—it was really a form of invisible ink made a great deal redder to resemble blood. It was painted on the walls before we arrived, but until heat struck it—the words wouldn't show. Once I thought we were licked—when the words started to run. You see, we put the chemical into a colorless wax to make the letters stand out better when heat brought them into visible existence.

"That's why you boys were sweating so much. Remember that the words appeared just above a radiator? We had to have a lot of heat. These blood-stains on the floor — they're caused the same way. There are men in the cellar who followed the path we created and heated the floor until the stuff showed. It was tough going in that house by the public dump. We had to spread ashes around to cover the footprints we made. That was real blood I smeared on your hand though. I cut my finger to get it."

"But—but how did you know them four hideouts?" Judel gasped.

"Grogan was a good cop and good cops file reports every day," Kennedy said. He recorded those four places just in case something happened to him. We checked up, found the bullet holes here and set our trap. Unless you confessed, we had nothing on you whether we found Grogan's corpse or not. We needed both the confession and the body. We saw faint marks where you'd dragged the body out and we arranged the blood spots accordingly."

"Fooled," Judel groaned. Then he kicked at Varno and cursed. "If it hadn't been for this mug, I'd never have fallen, but he was supposed to be a tough guy. When he cracked, I figured there was something to it."

"Take them out," Kennedy sighed. "And Judel—you'll know very soon whether or not there are ghosts. The electric chair will provide the means."

SALLY the SLEUTH

by Charles Barr

"DIRTY POLITICS"

SEVERAL TIMES, IN COMPROMISING PLACES, A GIRL WOULD PLANT HERSELF ON MY LAP AND SOMEBODY WOULD SNAP A PICTURE. IT IS ALL PART OF MURDOCK'S PLAN TO GET A STOOGE OF HIS ELECTED TO MY POST.

LEAVE IT TO US, JUDGE.
YOU MUST CLEAR ME IN THIS PICTURE MESS —AND FAST. REMEMBER, THE ELECTION IS ONE WEEK OFF!

AFTER THE JUDGE LEAVES...
MURDOCK MAY TRY TO FRAME THE JUDGE WITH MORE PICTURES. SALLY, YOU'VE GOT TO FIND OUT WHO THE PHOTOGRAPHER IS.

SALLY VISITS MURDOCK'S "SHAMROCK" BAR...
SHAMROCK BAR

INSIDE, SALLY PICKS UP A GIRL ...
CRIPES! I NEED A DRINK!
HAVE JOE MIX YOU A "SHAMROCK SPECIAL". IT PACKS A WALLOP.

THIS IS A WOW! —AND I NEED IT, THE WAY I FEEL—
WATSA MATTER, KID, IN TROUBLE?

OH, I JUST GOT OUT OF THE PEN, WHERE THAT LOUSE, JUDGE GRAY, SENT ME FOR SHOPLIFTING!
YOU OUGHTA MEET PETE MURDOCK. HE'S A RIGHT GUY AND HE CAN HELP YOU.

HELLO, PETE. THIS LITTLE GIRL GOT A RAW DEAL FROM JUDGE GRAY. MAYBE YOU CAN FIND SOME WORK FOR HER.
HIYA, MAE. WE CAN USE HER IF SHE'S SMART. COME BACK TOMORROW.

SALLY REPORTS TO THE CHIEF...
SO FAR, SO GOOD, SALLY. KEEP THAT APPOINTMENT TOMORROW, AND REMEMBER, WE WANT TO KNOW WHO TAKES THE PICTURES.

NEXT DAY, IN MURDOCK'S OFFICE ...
HI, MR. MURDOCK. HERE I AM!
OKAY, TOOTS. NOW YOU CAN GET EVEN WITH JUDGE GRAY. THIS IS SAMMY. YOU AND HIM WORK AS A TEAM. NOW LISSEN—

THE JUDGE IS GOING TO SPEAK IN A REAL TOUGH SECTION THIS AFTERNOON. WHEN HE'S IN FRONT OF PADDY'S SALOON, YOU RUN UP AND GIVE HIM A BIG HUG — MAKE IT HOT! SAMMY'LL DO THE REST.
3

THAT AFTERNOON...
VOTE FOR GRAY
VOTE FOR GRAY

LATER, THE JUDGE PASSES PADDY'S...
OKAY—HERE WE GO!
PADDY'S BAR

SAMMY KNOCKS OFF THE JUDGES HAT...
WHAT THE—?

I. SAY—STOP IT!
PADDY'S BAR

SAMMY AND SALLY HURRY AWAY...
I'M GOING TO MY APARTMENT TO DEVELOP THESE. WANNA COME UP, BABY?
SURE, I'D LIKE TO SEE YOU DEVELOP.

THAT'S MY DARKROOM. COME ON IN WITH ME.
SURE.
AFTER THE WORK IS DONE, SAMMY GETS OTHER IDEAS . . .
GIMME A KISS, BABY.
SURE, HANDSOME.
TRYING TO STEAL MY GUY, YOU HEEL!
MAE PAYS AN UNEXPECTED CALL . . .
MMM-DO IT AGAIN, SAMMY.
HEY - WHAT GOES ON HERE?
5

BREAK IT UP, YOU DAMES, OR WE'LL ALL GET IN TROUBLE WIT' MURDOCK!

I'LL BREAK YOUR HEAD, YOU DOUBLE CROSSING LOUSE!
MEANWHILE, I'M GETTING OUT OF HERE.

EVERYTHING IS AT SAMMY'S PLACE, CHIEF, 124 ELM STREET.
FINE, SALLY. WE'LL PAY HIM A VISIT.

BUT THAT NIGHT, JUDGE GRAY IS CHLOROFORMED AND KIDNAPPED ...

HE'LL BE FOUND HERE, IN FRONT OF PADDY'S JOINT.
REEKIN' WIT' BOOZE, BOSS. DIS'LL FIX HIS WAGON!

NEXT DAY, THERE ARE HEADLINES ...
WHAT'S THIS— "JUDGE GRAY FOUND DRUNK IN A LOW DIVE"
THAT'S NOT THE KIND OF MAN I'LL VOTE FOR.
I EITHER!

MURDOCK'S CANDIDATE GAINS FOLLOWERS...
FELLOW CITIZENS, YOU CANNOT ELECT A SOUSE AS JUDGE!
YOU'RE RIGHT!
HOORAY FOR BURNS!
VOTE FOR BURNS
VOTE FOR BURNS
VOTE FOR BURNS

SALLY, JUDGE GRAY IS ILL FROM THAT EXPERIENCE. WE'VE GOT TO ACT FAST TO CLEAR HIS NAME. FIRST, WE'LL GO AND SEE SAMMY.
I'M RIGHT WITH YOU, CHIEF.

PUT 'EM UP, YOU TWO!
WHAT'S DIS?
IT'S THAT GIRL! SHE RATTED ON US!

HERE ARE HIS PICTURES AND NEGATIVES. YOU TAKE THEM, SALLY, WHILE I TAKE THESE TWO TO THE HOOSEGOW.

THAT EVENING, AT A SCHEDULED RALLY FOR JUDGE GRAY...
LADIES AND GENTLEMEN, I REGRET THAT JUDGE GRAY IS ILL AND WON'T BE ABLE TO SPEAK THIS EVENING -
"ILL", MY EYE! HE'S STILL DRUNK!
WHAT CAN YOU EXPECT OF A MAN LIKE THAT?
7

THE CHIEF RISES IN THE AUDIENCE...
JUST A MINUTE, FOLKS. I HAVE SOME NEWS FOR YOU—

JUDGE GRAY WAS FRAMED WITH PHONEY PICTURES BY PETE MURDOCK. THEN MURDOCK KIDNAPED THE JUDGE AND SATURATED HIS CLOTHES WITH LIQUOR... ALL TO GET HIS OWN MAN INTO OFFICE SO AS TO CONTINUE THE REIGN OF THE UNDERWORLD IN YOUR FAIR CITY. I'M HAPPY TO TELL YOU THAT MURDOCK AND HIS WHOLE MOB IS NOW IN THE CITY JAIL FACING A LONG LIST OF SERIOUS CHARGES. YOU MAY HAVE FULL CONFIDENCE IN JUDGE GRAY.

SALLY GIVES THE JUDGE A HAND...
SURE YOU FEEL WELL ENOUGH, JUDGE?
YES, I'LL MAKE IT, SALLY, THANKS TO YOU.

HERE COMES JUDGE GRAY, NOW!
WE'RE FOR YOU, JUDGE!
WE'RE FOR YOU, GRAY!

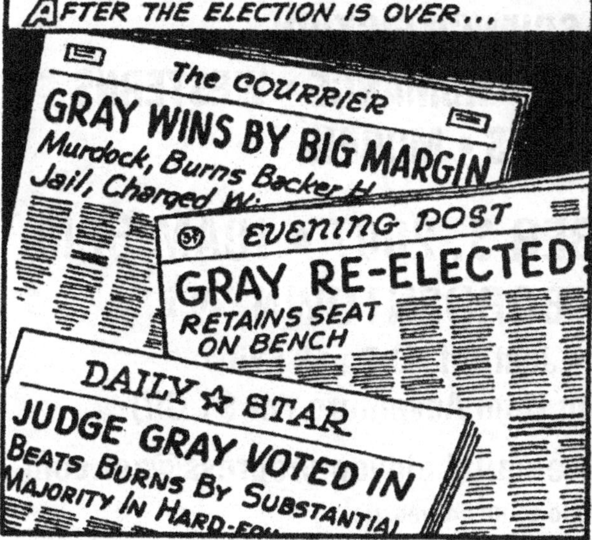
AFTER THE ELECTION IS OVER...
The COURRIER
GRAY WINS BY BIG MARGIN
Murdock, Burns Backer In Jail, Charged W...
EVENING POST
GRAY RE-ELECTED!
RETAINS SEAT ON BENCH
DAILY STAR
JUDGE GRAY VOTED IN
Beats Burns By Substantial Majority In Hard-fou...

I'M DEEPLY GRATEFUL TO YOU BOTH. THEY'D HAVE GOTTEN AWAY WITH THE ELECTION IF YOU HADN'T CLEARED ME.
SALLY GETS THE CREDIT, JUDGE. SHE'S A GREAT GAL!
FOLLOW SALLY IN PRIVATE DETECTIVE

PULP ADVENTURECON #7

Thousands Of Pulp Magazines,
Vintage Paperbacks & Paper Ephemra For Sale

MYSTERY • SCIENCE FICTION
SUPER-HEROES • HORROR • ROMANCE • WESTERNS
CLASSIC FILMS • MORE!!

SATURDAY, NOVEMBER 3, 2007 • 10AM-5PM
RAMADA INN • BORDENTOWN, NJ

(1083 Route 206) • Just Off NJ Trnpk Exit 7

Admission: $6 (Mention High Adventure For $1 Off)

www.boldventurepress.com • email: boldventurepress@aol.com

• More info to come on website

Subscribe

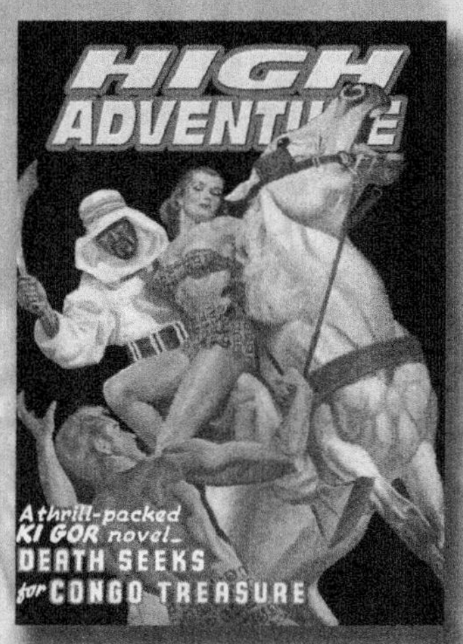

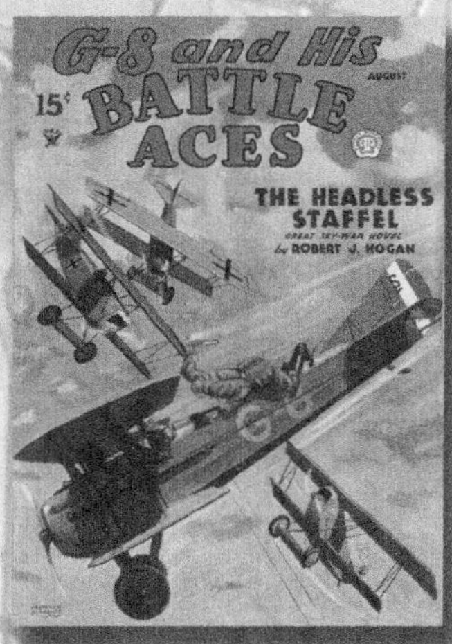

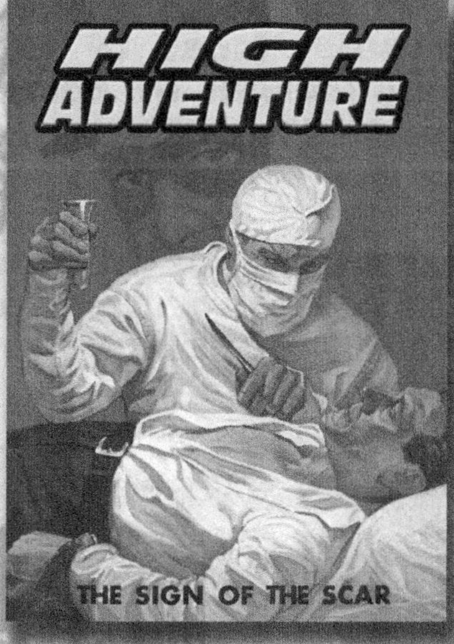

G-8 and His Battle Aces
4 Issues - $40.00

High Adventure
6 Issues - $45.00

Adventure House - 914 Laredo Road - Silver Spring, MD 20901
sales@adventurehouse.com - www.adventurehouse.com

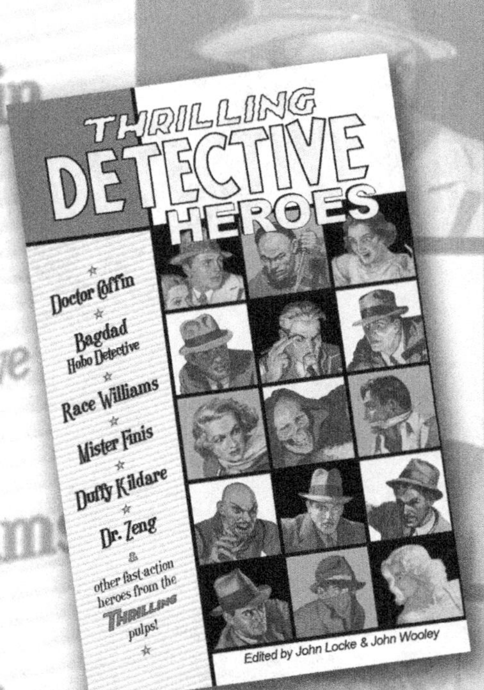

Thrilling Detective Heroes

From the '30s through the '50s, madmen, mayhem, and the murder ruled the malignant world of the Thrilling detective pulps. To the rescue came a succession of intrepid investigators fearing nothing but injustice. These were the Thrilling Detective Heroes. Some of their names are legend in pulpdom. Most of them remain to be discovered in this collection of colorful tales taken from Thrilling's flagship detective pulps, THRILLING DETECTIVE and POPULAR DETECTIVE.

Each story features a series hero in one of his most entertaining exploits. The detectives range from the flamboyant figures of the '30s to the hardboiled, hard-bitten private dicks of the late-'40s.

6x9
276 pages
Edited by John Locke
and John Wooley
$20.00

HIGH ADVENTURE
KI-GOR
HIGH ADVENTURE
HIGH ADVENTURE
DAYS OF Creation
An Amazing Curtis Newton Novel
By BRETT STERLING

Made in the USA
Monee, IL
07 July 2026

56552460R00063